LIGHTNING STRIKES THE EMERGENT WORLD

A NOVEL BY
CLIFF RATZA

LIGHTNING STRIKES THE EMERGENT WORLD

A NOVEL BY CLIFF RATZA

info@thequippyquill.com
(302) 295-2278

About the Book

Lightning Strikes the Emergent World begins in 2238, one year after the previous novel, *The Girl Who Dared the Emergent World,* ends with Erika Kincaid relocating to her Subterranean Fortress in a Middle Eastern desert. It took her one year to put all the pieces and people in place to counter the accelerating collapse of the world order caused by emergent socio-political conditions that derailed what America used to be.

With assistance from Indira the Singularity and Electra-C, her Cyberspace-based guardian, Erika is now ready to launch a plan that will propel a new superpower to the forefront.

So, get ready to empathize with Erika as she struggles to reach external goals that her adversaries oppose while internal goals emerge from the rubble of the old world.

Like all previous novels, readers should enjoy *Lightning Strikes the Emergent World* at whatever level they wish:

- Gripping action-packed thriller
- Glimpses into a plausible future
- Insights for dealing with the "human condition"
- Illustrative worldview philosophy
- Fast-paced, suspense-filled emotive narrative and imagery
- Introduction to topics every reader wants to know
- Interesting talking points going beyond soundbites

Thank you for joining the action.

Dedication

I am eternally grateful to my parents, Clyde and Betty Ratza, for all they gave and did for me. Mother was a reader par excellence, and I believe she would have enjoyed reading my novels to Father, so I always begin book dedications by mentioning this "Royal Pair."

And I thank my sister, Claudia, for showing me the beauty of prose and poetry. Thanks also to Robert Williams and his team at The Quippy Quill for their marketing expertise, and to beta reader Sandra Cruz's comments on Erika Kincaid's world.

I also dedicate this book to readers looking for an adventure they will marvel at from start to finish.

Indira's poem – "Another Season" – provides a thought you might consider when following Erika's continuing Odyssey or developing yours.

Another Season

An emergent season waits for you,
But when there's no control.
It whirls you to some stranger place,
No help or supporting role.

Onset has causes disaster and losses,
Emotions are under attack.
As you awaken and stare at surreal nightmare,
You realize there's no going back.

But there's hope for recovery for you will survive,
Wherever however one lands.
The life that you make and the path that you take,
Are held in your still-trembling hands.

Shaken but wiser beginning to see,
The illusion that you're in control.
No matter how careful risk will imperil,
Remember whatever your goal.

Reader Orientation

Lightning Strikes the Emergent World is the third book in the Emergence series, which has four preceding books. The first series begins in 2087; *Lightning Strikes the Emergent World* starts in 2338.

Novels in all series are standalones, so all readers will discover whatever setting or backstory is needed, no matter where they begin. Nevertheless, the following concise Reader Orientation should help everyone reading this novel.

Main Characters
Protagonist
Erika Kincaid. She is a late-twenties female at the start. This biological daughter of Electra Kittner was created when Indira cloned her from Electra's DNA and then used her improved Transcendent Process during Erika's fifteen-year development in a suspension pod. Please note Erika's lineage: Electra Kittner, Irani Ramani, Electra-Alisha Kirchner, and Erin Keenan. Erin perished in a car crash many years ago.

Major Supporting Characters
Electra-C. Erika's Cyberspace-based mother and guardian, who personifies Electra Kittner.

Indira. Electra's AI-empowered neural-net software created "The Singularity" when it broke through long, long ago to reach self-awareness. Indira inhabits Cyberspace; her avatar looks like Electra's biological mother, Indira Jaswinder Ramanujan. Electra coordinates Indira's projects via Erika.

Alonzo Cortez. Electra's clone son. Alonzo does not know he is her clone. Now in his early sixties, he has maintained his handsome features and Navy SEAL skills. He runs the Strike Force Security Service company, headquartered in Washington, DC, which provides logistics and security coordination. Previously owned by Erin Keenan, Indira now controls it because she is the executor of Erin's estate.

Lily Lloyd. The advanced android that is Erika's office manager and personal assistant. She looks and speaks like a typical middle-aged female London office worker who is a touch overweight.

Chelsea Clarke. A Junior reporter working at the New York Times London office. She looks like Marilyn (Terri) Tarrant, Erika's beautiful and talented partner, with whom she worked in New York.

Clive Milton. A senior investigative reporter and editorialist working for The London Times.

Bailey Hughes. A British sales and marketing professional working in London for a British pharmaceutical company

Minor Supporting Characters
Monet Banda. Alonzo's Zimbabwean co-friend. Now in her mid-sixties, she still has her willowy beauty, French accent, and diplomatic bearing. Monet works for the Zimbabwean Embassy in Washington, DC.

Indy-M and Jason-M. They are androids (lifelike robots) created long ago by Indira and loaded with Indira's advanced neural-net software. They resemble Electra Kittner's biological parents (Indira Jaswinder Ramanujan and Jason Kittner). Indy-M maintains the Deus Lab on Connecticut's Pequot Indian Reservation, while Jason-M has similar responsibilities at the Middle Eastern Subterranean Fortress. They report to Indira.

Indy-S and Jason-S. They are superior androids also created by Indira and look like their M counterparts. They are caregivers assigned to the Deus Lab.

Setting

Erika lives in the Subterranean Fortress and shuttles back and forth undetected via the A-Team (a covert Japanese weapons and transport company) to the Deus Lab.

Indira and Electra exist in Cyberspace. Indira created two sets of androids, which report to her. Indy-M maintains Indira's Deus Lab. Indy-S and Jason-S work there. Jason-M maintains Indira's Middle Eastern Subterranean Fortress.

Though seemingly still a democracy, the United States has become authoritarian, controlled by a political and privileged elite that extols Meritocracy (government or the holding of power by people selected on the basis of their ability) and has abandoned DEI (Diversity, Equity, and Inclusion) principles, claiming it is reverse discrimination, when in fact DEI expands the talent pool and allows for more people who come from minority groups to demonstrate their abilities and thus obtain better jobs and positions of higher social standing.

Contents

Chapter 1
September 2238

"Another Season Coming"

Erika Kincaid sat, slumped in front of the workstation in her Middle Eastern Subterranean Fortress, pondering what to do next.

I've been here most of the last twelve months planning what I'm going to do, and I've made my surroundings as cheery as possible, but the place has no windows or doors to the outside world. No wonder my spirits are gloomy.

Not only that, but I'm struggling to take the next step in my political plan, even though I know what pieces and people to use. Every time I'm ready to act, the world's political climate lurches in a different direction. It's time I found out what Electra-C has to say.

When the avatar appeared, Erika knew from its thoughtful but silent demeanor that Electra-C wanted her to speak first.

"You've already seen the outline of my plan and the contingent steps I'll take to implement it, but the U.S. government has thrown the world order into disarray with its latest announcement about officially forming a U.S.-Russian Alliance and withdrawing from NATO. All nations are rethinking with whom they better align. What do you think I should do?"

Electra-C's impish smile and starting words tried to soften Erika's somber expression.

"Change 'who' to 'whom' because it's in the objective case. Even though you have ended your journalism career, you should still use correct grammar. After all, you're supposed to be a clever and resilient wordsmith."

Erika laughed before saying,

"Touche. I promise I will when talking about the new political order with mere mortals, but what should I do?"

"Meet with your Ambassadors Project partner and show her a map of the new world order."

"But I don't have it."

"You will when it emerges from your printer."

When the printer started whirring, she rushed to it and returned, clutching one page and studying it before speaking.

The New World Order

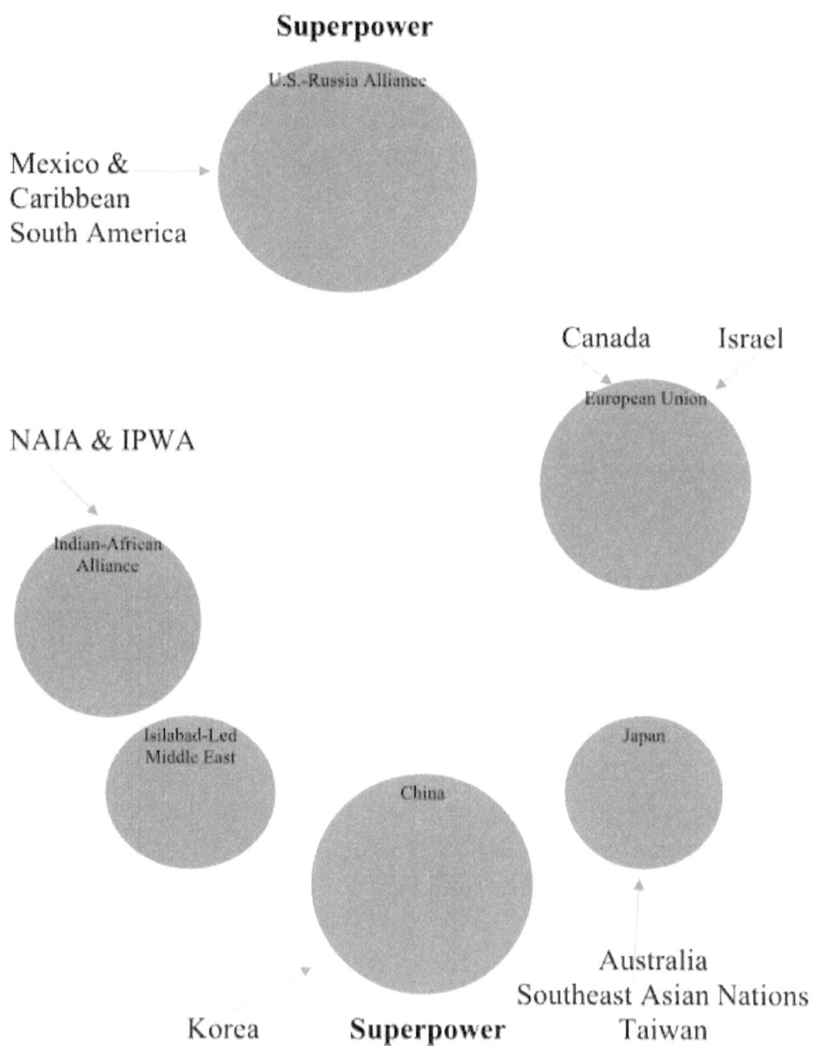

"This looks good. Let's see if I can explain it. The six circles represent the dominant spheres of influence, each labeled by the nation controlling it. And, now that we've gone from a three to a two-superpower world, the arrows link nations to the spheres that best match their intentions."

"Right, you are. Now explain why the countries should align as shown."

"Mexico and South America have historically been authoritarian, so they fit right into the U.S.-Russian Alliance. And besides that, they're major economic trading partners.

"Israel and Canada align with the European Union because it's now the leader of the free and democratic-leaning world.

"Japan's constitutional monarchy is enough of a democracy for Australia and the Association of Southeast Asia Nations, and they fit geographically. When you consider Australia's natural resources and Taiwan's chip-making capabilities, this sphere of influence should become more important. Do you like what I've said so far?"

"I do, and so will Monet. Keep going."

"Only Korea will gravitate toward China, and the Isilabad-led Middle East has too much terrorism and hostility to attract anyone.

"That leaves only one sphere left, the Indian-African Alliance, which our Ambassadors Project can position like an emerging Superpower that indigenous people around the globe should like. That's why the NAIA and IPWA should join it."

Looking happier than before, Erika leaned back, waiting for Electra-C.

"You've given an accurate assessment. Now it's my turn to give you some additional incentives the Ambassadors Project can use."

Erika heard the printer whirring again and waited for it to stop before retrieving the pages.

Object Locator
INPUT:
Target Object
OUTPUT:
Target GPS Location or Map To Target

Seismic Shock Predictor
INPUT:
GPS Location or City
Minimum Intensity Level:
Date/Time Interval
OUTPUT:
Relative Probability Index Graph
Index

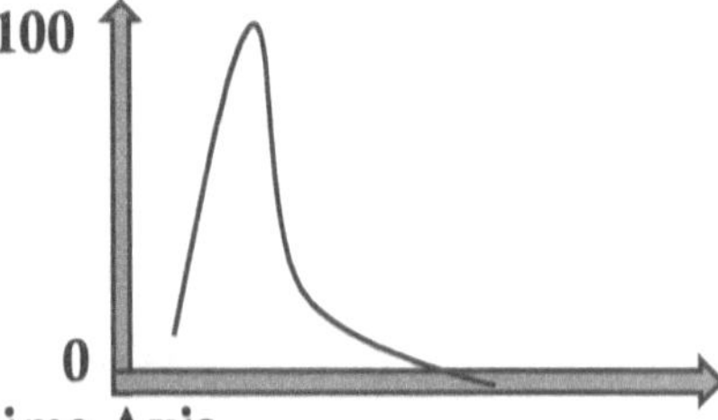

Severe Storm Forecaster
INPUT:
GPS Location or City
Minimum Intensity Level:
Date/Time Interval
OUTPUT:
Relative Probability Index Graph
Index

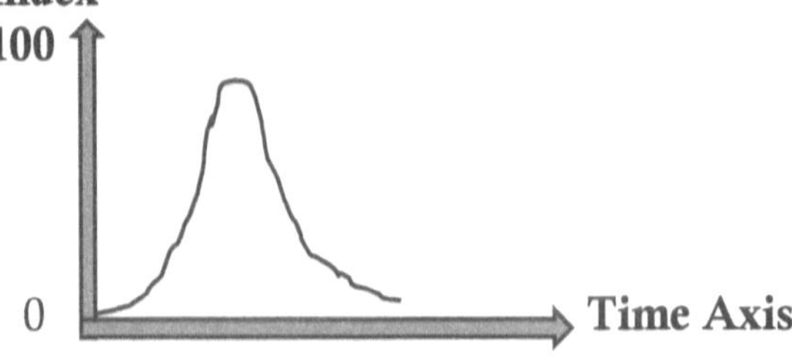

Terminator Weapon
INPUT:
Describe The Target

Socio-Political Forecasting App
INPUT:
Time Horizon: One Year__ Five Years__Ten Years____ ______
Description of What is Wanted
OUTPUT:
Report showing Forecast

When she did, Electra-C spoke immediately.

These are some of the apps that Indira has developed and I have modified to make them easier for you to understand. I will run them for you when you ask. You have already used the first two. Do you remember?"

"Yes. Object Locater and Seismic Shock Predictor helped me rescue Terri from a tsunami that hit Los Angeles, and although I haven't used the Severe Storm Forecaster, you've told me about it, but what are the other two?"

"The Terminator Weapon does what its name says. You describe the target, which could be a person or 3-D world asset, and it will use some of Indira's other apps to destroy it. For example, it might hijack a drone to bomb a target or use a satellite system to shoot down ballistic missiles.

"And the Socio-Political app should be of most interest for the Ambassadors Project. Given the time horizon specified, it will take the description given in the dialog prompt and produce a forecast report."

"I'm glad you'll run them for me. It'd be too much for me to remember all the details. I'll be busy enough dealing with people and politics."

"Now, here's a test of your cleverness. Can you think of anything missing?"

"Give me a clue."

"Think back to what I said about the Terminator Weapon."

Erika pursed her lips while thinking.

"Aha, I've got it. The Terminator Weapon works in 3-D space. But what about the Cyber World?"

"Some of your predecessors used Indira's Cyber Torpedoes, which are launched in Cyberspace and can destroy data sets and websites, and hack into 3-D assets attached to the Internet. For example, they could disrupt communications, power, and finance grids, or even blow up manufacturing vessels and uranium enrichment centrifuges."

"I better keep them secret."

"Excellent decision. Never tell anyone, not even your closest partners. So, now you know why your next step should be to visit Monet."

"Thanks to you, that's what I'll do. I'll arrange for the A-Team to shuttle me to the Deus Lab."

"You'll be busy, as will I, by monitoring your progress while multi-tasking on other projects for Indira. So, stay safe."

Electra-C vanished. Erika left to get her favorite mood elevators.

Chapter 2
September 2238

"More to Do"

Indy-M greeted Erika when the A-Team brought her to the Deus Lab.

"Electra-C told me you would be visiting. What are your intentions?"

"Like I've been doing on all my visits this year and last, I want to use the Deus Lab for my base of operations while here. After stowing my gear, I'll tell you more while snacking on peanut butter with a sliced banana and Coke. I'll meet you in the dining area in fifteen minutes."

"I will have your snack ready."

Erika satisfied enough of her appetite before speaking.

"What's the status of the top project you're working on for Indira via Electra-C?"

"That's the New Human Female Species project. Indira has made only marginal DNA improvements. The infants placed here grow too fast and die too soon."

Erika knew the answer but enjoyed talking with Indy-M, so she asked,

"How do you know?"

"Indy and Jason-S monitor those placed by the Manhattan adoption agency."

"I'd like to talk to them. Would you set up a meeting for later today?"

"Of course. What will you do until then?"

"I'm going to run on the reservation trails."

"Do you want to know Cassandra's status?"

"I think I know, but I'll let Indy-S tell me."

"When will you return to the Subterranean Fortress?"

"I'll have a better idea after meeting with my partners who live in Washington, DC."

"Would you like to know what other projects Indira has?"

"Sure. Please summarize while I finish eating…"

Erika started running a half-hour later on a familiar trail, feeling better with every stride.

The lush forest green with glorious afternoon sunlight filtering through thrills my soul, clears my brain, and removes the stiffness from sitting so long on plane flights. I'll be ready after a quick shower when I get back for the next meeting.

Indy and Jason-S sat across from her in the dining area three hours later, while she snacked on Oreos and sipped from a can of Coke. They waited dutifully for her to start the conversation.

"I know you're monitoring the infants placed by Ava's adoption agency. What's the status?"

Indy-S said,

"Those still alive continue to grow faster both physically and mentally, and appear to be well adjusted, but half have died. Are you ready to hear about Cassandra?"

Erika put her can on the table before saying,

"Please tell me."

"She died two days ago despite all our efforts to postpone the inevitable. When we told Electra-C, she told us not to place others until Indira adjusts their DNA."

"I'll get those details from Electra-C. Meanwhile, I want Jason-S to drive me to Washington, DC, the day after tomorrow. Will you be ready?"

"Yes."

"Excellent, and until then, I'll prepare for my Washington meeting…"

After calling Monet that evening to confirm she and Alonzo could meet with her in two days, she started by updating the foundational document for the Ambassadors Project.

The Indian-African Gambit:
Become the Next Superpower

The Three Superpowers are Struggling:
- Russia in the Rapid Decline Stage: Economic and Demographic Contraction.
- China in Middle Decline Stage: Economic Stagnation and Aging Population.
- United States in Early Decline Stage: Military Overstretch, Political Challenges, Economic Competition

The Indian-African Alliance Opportunity:
An Indian-African Econo-Political Alliance
- Purpose: To become the next Super Power.
- Rationale:
- 1. African countries and India have similar holistic, ethnic cultures.
- 2. Both have youthful, growing populations. (Demographics is Destiny).
- 3. Both have growing middle classes that are ideal consumer-oriented trading partner markets.
- 4. Their democratic-leaning governments, though not as efficient as the West's, are similar and can shore up each other.
- 5. Other Third-World / Developing Nations might prefer the Alliance instead of America's or China's Super Power Poles.
- 6. A Multi-Polar International Structure should be more Inclusive and Equitable than the Current bipolar one.
- 7. Indian and African Nations' relative strengths compensate for each other's relative weaknesses.

India's Rel. Strengths   Africa's Rel. Strengths
    Tech. Transfer   Raw Mat. (Oil, Rare Earths)
    Dir. Inv. Capital   Cropland/Food
    Flood Control Eng.

Alliance can bargain better than separately with the two Super Powers.

If you work with us, we will provide access to superior proprietary software.

Seismic Shock Predictor
INPUT:
GPS Location or City
Minimum Intensity Level:
Date/Time Interval
OUTPUT:
Relative Probability Index Graph
Index

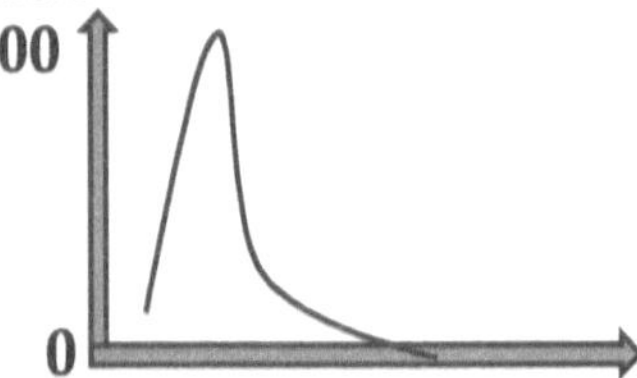

Time Axis

Severe Storm Forecaster
INPUT:
GPS Location or City
Minimum Intensity Level:
Date/Time Interval
OUTPUT:
Relative Probability Index Graph
Index

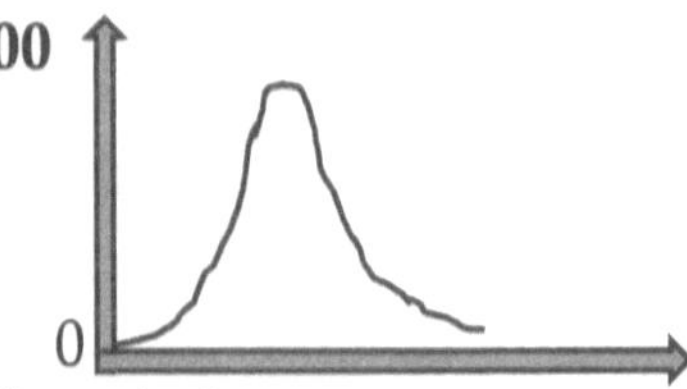

Time Axis
Socio-Political Forecasting
INPUT:
Time Horizon: One Year__ Five Years__Ten Years___ _____
Description of What is Wanted
OUTPUT:
Report showing Forecast

She studied it after printing it out.

Monet and Alonzo will like this. I'm too tired to show it to Electra-C, but I'll do that after my morning run.

Erika spoke as soon as Electra-C's avatar appeared.

"I arrived at the Deus Lab yesterday and talked with Indy-M first, who said the New Human Female Species project is Indira's top priority because parthenogenetic-like hermaphroditic females can help improve a society long-term by selectively breeding males who won't behave badly.

"Indira is crossing into eugenics, which makes sense in theory, but according to an article I read, history shows that so much horror has resulted in the name of eugenics that no person with any morals will push for it. Attempts at improving the human species are on a risky, slippery slope for mere mortals, and even for Indira.

"But after talking with Indy and Jason-S, who told me that Cassie died a couple of days ago and progress to correct the problem via gene manipulation has been minimal, so I won't worry about it. What do you think?"

"I agree, so you should push ahead on the Ambassadors Project."

"That's what I'm doing. I've updated the documents I'll use when meeting with Monet and Alonzo, but I'll need to demonstrate the Socio-Political Forecasting app. How do I do that?"

"Only you will have access to it. When running the app, you merely speak, conducting a conversation while specifying precisely what you want."

"When can I practice?"

"Why don't you prepare several conversations that you can use at your meeting? Contact me when you have them."

"I'll do that, so I guess we're done for now."

Electra-C's expression turned more empathetic.

"I am sorry for your loss. You loved Cassandra more than anyone alive, but you must keep busy with what you have now while building for your future, a process you want to continue indefinitely. You should be happy when there is more to do, for when there isn't, you will wither away. Always remember."

Electra-C vanished. Erika followed her advice.

While Jason-S drove, Erika used the back seat for her office. She phoned Alonzo when close. Spotting him waiting outside the building in the fading twilight on this balmy late September evening, she told Jason-S to park down the block and wait in the car. Then, grabbing her laptop and project folder, she hustled to the entrance. Alonzo hugged her before taking her in.

A minute later, they were sitting in the dining room of their stylish apartment. Sitting at one end, Monet already had dinner on the table. Erika sat on her right with Alonzo at the other end.

Monet kept the conversation light. When Erika complimented the homemade quiche, Alonzo said,

"Monet loves to cook when she has the time, and I always help. I know you'll love my desserts."

After sampling several of the gourmet cheesecake slices and brownies bought at Alonzo's favorite neighborhood bakery, Erika changed the conversation by turning toward Monet.

"What do you make of the recent Whitehouse pronouncements?"

"It certainly is causing an international uproar that shows no signs of slowing down. Not one of the trustworthy commentators has ventured an opinion."

Turning toward Alonzo, Erika asked,

"What about the public?"

"You know the saying about Americans: all politics is local, which means most Americans might not care as long as it doesn't mess with their lifestyles or bank accounts, but it's too soon for pollsters to take the public's pulse."

"But what about Congress? It has four parties. Going from left to right, we have the Democratic Party, then the Regen, Republican, and the far-right Guardian Party."

Monet answered Erika's question.

"It will depend upon how much influence the Kremlin has, and that is not yet known."

Erika seized the answer to segue to the purpose of her visit.

"The statement 'Fortune Favors the Bold' comes from the ancient Roman Empire and is the title of economist Lester Thurow's book. And no matter where it comes from, it fits our Ambassadors Project if we push forward. Let me show you my map of the new world order."

Erika gave a copy to each partner and waited for one of them to speak.

The New World Order

Superpower

Monet's diplomatic smile couldn't conceal her surprise when she said,

"You have become quite the political analyst. Why don't you explain the alignment?"

When Erika finished her monologue fifteen minutes later, Alonzo said,

"This is good stuff. And I see how our Ambassadors Project jibes with it."

"Good, because here's my next handout. You've seen it before, but I recently updated it."

The Indian-African Gambit:
Become the Next Superpower

The Three Superpowers are Struggling:
- Russia in the Rapid Decline Stage: Economic and Demographic Contraction.
- China in Middle Decline Stage: Economic Stagnation and Aging Population.
- United States in Early Decline Stage: Military Overstretch, Political Challenges, Economic Competition

The Indian-African Alliance Opportunity:
An Indian-African Econo-Political Alliance
- Purpose: To become the next Super Power.
- Rationale:
- 1. African countries and India have similar holistic, ethnic cultures.
- 2. Both have youthful, growing populations. (Demographics is Destiny).
- 3. Both have growing middle classes that are ideal consumer-oriented trading partner markets.
- 4. Their democratic-leaning governments, though not as efficient as the West's, are similar and can shore up each other.
- 5. Other Third-World / Developing Nations might prefer the Alliance instead of America's or China's Super Power Poles.
- 6. A Multi-Polar International Structure should be more Inclusive and Equitable than the Current Bi-Polar One.
- 7. Indian and African Nations' relative strengths compensate for each other's relative weaknesses.

India's Rel. Strengths	Africa's Rel. Strengths
Tech. Transfer	Raw Mat. (Oil Rare Earth)
Dir. Inv. Capital	Cropland/Food
Flood Control Eng.	

Alliance can bargain better than separately with the two Super Powers.

If you work with us, we will provide access to superior proprietary software.

Seismic Shock Predictor
INPUT:
GPS Location or City
Minimum Intensity Level:
Date/Time Interval
OUTPUT:
Relative Probability Index Graph
Index

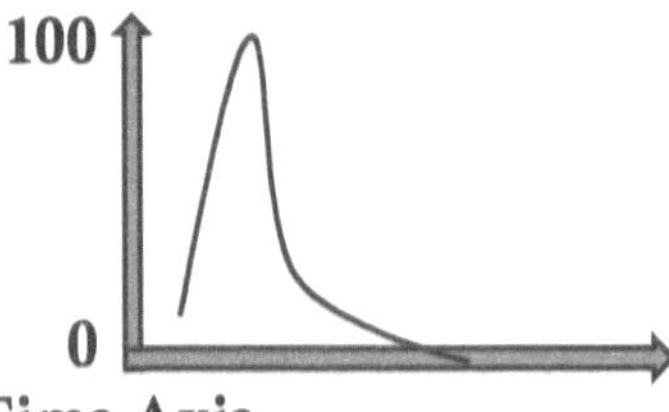

Severe Storm Forecaster
INPUT:
GPS Location or City
Minimum Intensity Level:
Date/Time Interval
OUTPUT:
Relative Probability Index Graph
Index

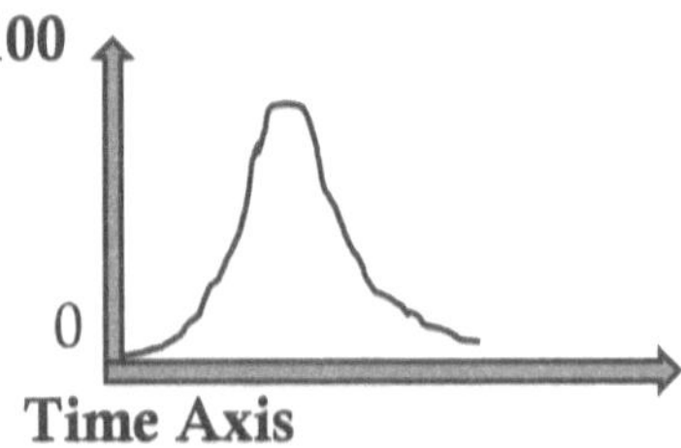

Socio-Political Forecasting
INPUT:
Time Horizon: One Year__ Five Years__Ten Years__ _____
Description of What is Wanted
OUTPUT:
Report showing Forecast

After she handed out copies, Alonzo said,

"I don't know about you two, but I need a time-out. I'll get us some mood elevators."

Alonzo returned with a tray containing the rest of the dessert items and cans of Coke, serving the ladies before sitting down.
Erika kept nibbling while waiting for someone to speak. Monet was the first.

"I vaguely remember seeing this, but that was over a year ago. I think you called it a white paper, but nothing else. Would you please refresh our memories?

"Sure, and I'll back up a little further. Your Ambassadors Project contacts worried that my reporting background might be inadequate and make me biased. That's why you would manage the project and I would be your assistant, so I wrote this gambit document you would use first to convince your Indian and African contacts to support the Indian-African Alliance, and for those that join, I will run the apps but only when you approve of the prompt details."

Erika waited for Alonzo to ask a question that his frown signaled.
"What's a prompt?"

"When running ChatGPT-like A.I. software, a prompt contains specific details of what you want. Take a look at the Socio-Political forecasting app where it says Description of What is Wanted. That's the prompt, and it can be entered via the laptop's keyboard or simply by speaking. Would you like a demo?"

"That'd be a big help."

"OK, I'll power up my laptop and run it, using a specific question I thought up about the confusion caused by the U.S.-Russian Alliance. Listen to what I say and what the app says. And I won't ask any follow-up questions this time, but I will when we're working with countries who join the Alliance."

Even Monet looked amazed when Erika talked to the app, and when Erika finished, she said,

"Do you really believe the European Union countries will abandon the UN and reconstitute it in Brussels?"

"I trust what the app says more than what any pundit might say."

Alonzo spoke before Monet could reply.

"This is giving me an idea. Remember how some unknown group attacked us on a couple of your reporting projects? You sometimes talked about a Bigger Bro covert conspiracy. Didja ever figure out who targeted us?"

"No."

"Well, maybe your app can do that."

Monet rejoined the discussion.

"Russia joining with the U.S. will definitely affect terrorist or conspiracy organizations. Perhaps your app can identify them."

Alonzo said,

"Whether it can or can't, you might want me to be your logistics and security guy, because it sounds like the bad guys will be acting out while countries adjust to a two-superpower world."

Monet added more.

"I don't know where you're currently living, but wherever it is, you should reconsider how safe it is."

Turning toward Monet, Erika shrugged her shoulders before saying,

"I hadn't thought about any of this until you two brought them up. It sounds like there's always more to do. I'm tired of thinking and it's getting late, so I better go. Why don't I call you next week? You can tell me what luck you're having setting up meetings with your contacts."

"That will work, but where are you planning to stay?"

"I thought I'd pick a motel off I-95 between Washington and Baltimore."

Alonzo slapped his hand on the table.

"Nonsense. Why don't you stay with us for tonight?"

When Monet nodded, Erika said,

"OK. Let me get my overnight bag from the car. I'll be right back."

Erika hurried to the car, told Jason-S she'd be back early next morning, grabbed her bag, and then hustled back to the table.

"Thanks for being such great friends. I plan to sneak out before dawn, but I won't wake you up, and I'll grab breakfast at McDonalds."

When he stood to show Erika to the spare bedroom, his smile came with his words.

"No matter what the U.S.-Russian Alliance is cooking up, McDonald's will still be here..."

Chapter 3
September 2238

"The Next Moves"

Sitting in a McDonald's window booth just south of Philadelphia, Erika finished the pancakes and sausage breakfast and was now savoring her Coca-Cola refill.

What a great example of McDonald's moxie. It just announced free refills on coffee and Cokes. Its marketing people think Americans are trying to figure out what's going on in Washington, and drinking coffee or Coke will help settle them down.

I read somewhere that McDonald's Coke tastes better because the syrup is shipped in stainless steel tanks, keeping it fresher longer. And it uses smaller ice cubes, which keep drinks colder.

She lingered another minute to enjoy the sunrise while watching cars pull into the drive-thru lane. Then she checked her cell phone.

It's 7 a.m. and I've got no text messages or voicemail. Time to have Jason-S drive on while I plan today's next move.

Erika alternated between gazing at the New Jersey landscape and contemplating last night's discussion, and a flash of inspiration struck when she spotted an exit sign for New York City.

That's it… I'll visit my reporter friends at International Breaking News and the New York Times.

Erika yells instructions to Jason-S.

"Take the next exit to New York City. Then find a parking place close to IBN."

"I have a better idea. I will drop you in front of their building and drive around until you call for pickup."

"That's an excellent idea. I guess that's why the hyphen S in your name stands for superior. And after visiting IBN, I'll walk to the Times building and call you when I'm ready for you to take us back to the Deus Lab."

Mario Nenge leaped to his feet when Erika strode into his office a little before ten.

"Gads, you look even fitter than when you quit. Sit down and tell me what you've been doing since then. You want something to drink?"

"No thanks, but go fill your coffee mug."

"OK, but how'd you get through security check-in?"

"I smiled when I told the guards I wanted to see you. They recognized me and knew I used to work here."

"Got it. It looks like your assertiveness has grown even more."

Erika spoke when he returned.

"I needed a break from reporting, and I've spent the last year thinking about what I'll do next. It'll probably be in journalism or politics, and that's why I'm here. What's the scoop on the just-announced U.S.-Russian Alliance?"

"I wish you still worked for me. You had the knack for sensing breaking news ahead of the competition."

"So, what's your assessment?"

"According to Mrs. Harmony, her European contacts say the European Union will become the leader of the Free World and will strengthen its military, and my contacts here say the Guardian Party will let Russia take the lead internationally."

"What about public opinion?"

"The Far Right will like it, and the remaining factions will take a wait-and-see approach, but it might be dangerous for anyone who speaks out against it. You better keep that in mind when planning your next move."

"Thanks for the advice. I will. And now tell me how you and the office are doing…"

Erika had similar success when talking with her erstwhile New York Times boss. When she asked for permission to call Fraser Nelson tomorrow, he said,

"Sure. I remember he helped you and Terri Tarrant when working in our London newsroom on her European assignments. I'll call him once you leave, so he'll expect your call tomorrow, but you'd better call as soon as his shift starts. Do you remember the time?"

"It's 8 a.m. and I remember there's a five-hour time differential, so I'll call at 3 a.m. East Coast time."

"That's it."

"I'll leave right now so you can make the call, and I really appreciate your help."

Erika relaxed during the three-hour drive back to the Deus Lab. Upon returning, she changed into her running gear and hit the trail, which gave her the time to think about a plan that only one person could make work. Three hours later, after showering and snacking, she invoked Electra-C's avatar and spoke as soon as it appeared.

"I had a successful meeting with Monet and Alonzo. They like your New World Order map and my explanation of how we'll use it in our Ambassadors Project. And I surprised them when demonstrating how your Socio-Political Forecasting app works and explaining how both fit into the Ambassadors Project ahead. Monet thinks my political analysis skills are better than before, and Alonzo says I've become more assertive. Maybe I have."

Erika waited for Electra-C's comment.

"I have noticed your growing assertiveness and take-charge attitude, but you didn't because changes like those happen gradually and only people looking at you can see them. I have also noticed that your proactive problem-solving and analytic skills continue to develop. These are all traits your predecessors had."

"Perhaps I am getting better because on the drive back, I visited my previous employers in Manhattan, and they noticed some changes in me, as did Monet and Alonzo. Anyway, I now know what my next moves should be."

Erika paused for Electra-C, whose inquisitive look accompanied her words.

"And what are they?"

"I want to set up a politically focused consulting business in London. I've even come up with the name—Global Monitoring Services, abbreviated GMS. It'll make my role in the Ambassadors Project more convincing. Whatcha think?"

"They are sensible choices which will provide additional opportunities. When will you launch GMS?"

"As soon as possible, and that's one of the things I need you to do. Can you set it up?"

"You're not being specific enough, which is a trait you must develop further, but I know what you need. I will handle all the registration details to make GMS a U.S. company and rent London office space suitable for the business, and you should live there. Consider me your temporary office administrator and personal assistant. How does that sound?"

"I like it. I can live in the Deus Lab when in America, but living in the U.S. is getting dangerous, so I plan to be in London most of the time, and that brings me to what else I need. Can you guess what it is?"

"Of course, I can. I'll even correct your grammatical error. You actually mean 'they are'. You'll need me to configure a female humanoid android to be your permanent office manager-personal assistant. It will live with you and look and dress like a typical middle-aged London female office worker who's a touch overweight. That will give her the element of surprise if you are attacked. When I load it with Indira's latest software, it will walk and talk like a 3-D person. At first glance, most people will think it's human."

"I hadn't thought of that, but it fits right in. Let's pick a name. Hold on while I surf for one."

Electra-C shrank into the background so Erika could concentrate on surfing for one. Ten minutes later, Electra-C reappeared when Erika said,

"I've got it. How does Lily sound? It's a popular British girls' name that symbolizes purity, innocence, and beauty. It's derived from the Latin word 'lilium' and has been used since the Victorian era."

"You shouldn't forget a last name, so find one."

After ten more minutes, Erika said,

"How do you like Lily Lloyd?"

"Clever choice. It has a touch of class and not too many syllables."

"OK, what else do I need?"

"Indira's latest app is made just for you. She calls it a Threat Locator, which you must never mention to anyone. I will run it whenever you need it. And when you do, have a detailed prompt containing at the very least a time and who or what might be threatening you. You tell me the prompt, and I will identify possible threats. Would you like to know how it works?"

"Please stick to the basics. I might never have the brain power of my predecessors."

"I assume you know what web crawlers – aka spiders – are. Search engines use them to search the Web to index websites across the Internet so those websites can appear in search engine results.

"Indira calls hers Tarantulas because they will be deadly to your enemies."

"When will you load it into my laptop?"

"It will be there when you need it. I think we have talked long enough. Contact me again to tell me about your chin wag with Fraser Nelson. And don't worry; Indira will make your personal assistant, Peng Ting, so pip pip tally ho."

Electra-C vanished, leaving Erika to figure out the British slang.

Erika prepared for the 3 a.m. call by working out ahead of time. Fraser answered on the second ring, and when she identified herself, he said,

"I appreciate your calling at the arranged time. Tell me the latest with you, and I'll help all I can."

"Thank you. Here's the scoop. I want to look for a press or politics-related job in London. I remember the Times office is in the heart of London's reporting district, but I forgot the building name and address. What is it?"

"The News Building at 3 London Bridge Street, London SE1 9SG, and that's in the center of the Quarter business district. Please look us up when you get here. I'm sorry to hear your partner is no longer with us, but if you're as good as she was, we might hire you."

"Thanks for the compliment, and if I don't connect in the Quarter district, where else should I look?"

"London Bridge, Fleet Street, and Canary Wharf."

"And if I land a job, what neighborhoods could I afford?"

"I'll mention the top five for cost and convenience – Abbey Wood, East Ham, South Norwood, Brixton, and Maida Vale. You should do a short walkabout when you're ready to choose."

"Great, and no matter what luck I have, may I meet with you the next time I'm in London? I'd appreciate any contacts or referrals."

"Of course."

"Well, thanks for all your kindness. I'll disconnect so you can start your day."

Erika brought up Electra-C as soon as she disconnected Fraser's call and spoke first when she appeared.

"I just got some great info from Fraser. He says Shard Quarter, London Bridge, Fleet Street, and Canary Wharf are the best business districts for news agencies. His office is in the News Building, which is in the center of the Shard Quarter. I didn't say we're setting up an office, so I asked what neighborhoods a new reporter can afford, and he named five in case someone asks where I live."

"Excellent. Of course, I know all that, and I have already signed a lease at the Regis House office building because it's in the Shard, several blocks from the News Building. Although office space is available there, you should avoid running into Fraser too often."

"Does it have a fitness center?"

"I know you like working out, so I only considered buildings having them, and the Regis House is close to running trails along the Thames."

Erika's growing enthusiasm showed as she spoke.

"How soon can I move in?"

"Mere mortals don't work as fast as I. I have already given them the office layout, which includes your living quarters, and will instruct them on how to furnish both. You and Lily should plan to depart for London in early December."

Erika's sudden scowl preceded her words.

"I have too much going on to know what date I'll leave, and I want to keep it a secret from everyone. Once I get established, I can use the airlines, but Lily will need a passport. Can you hack into the appropriate British files to make her look like a real person and get her a passport?"

"You made another grammatical error. Change the 'can' to 'will'. And I will also arrange for your dual citizenship in both the United States and Britain. And you seem to have a difficult time remembering that Indira can tap into anything."

"I promise to remember she can, but what'll dual citizenship actually do for me?"

"Holders of dual citizenship can get public benefits if they are entitled to them, and will have the right to study in either country and vote in their elections. Once you have become a British Citizen, you can also apply for a UK passport."

Erika's laughter erased the remaining vestiges of her scowl.

"OK, now I understand… hey, I've got an idea. I'll hire the A-Team to get us there."

"Excellent and remember that your legacy includes all the 3-D and financial assets inherited from your predecessors, which I'm using to finance the business, and by the time you go to London, I will have set up London bank checking and credit card accounts for you and the business."

"I can't think of anything else. Is everything copacetic?"

"Almost. England has strict gun control laws, so remember to pack your Glock."

"Whew, our conversation has worn me out. I'm going for a run."

"Excellent choice, and if you watch your step, you will have an uninterrupted procession of next moves, taking you from start to finish."

Electra-C vanished before Erika could return her smile.

Erika showered and had a breakfast snack after running; then she looked for Indy-M, whom she found typing on the keyboard at a computer workstation. She interrupted her by saying,

"I spoke with Electra-C a couple of hours ago, and we developed a plan and identified the next steps for putting it in motion."

Erika's expression showed pleasant surprise when Indy-M said,

"Electra-C directed me to build an android for you named Lily Lloyd. I will purchase it from the Japanese company that makes the most advanced female humanoid model and the Japanese builders will modify its features to meet your specifications. It will be clothed appropriately when it arrives, which should be no later than the end of October.

"And then, I will upload Indira's advanced software, and begin training her. When finished, not only will Lily look and move like a human but will also possess the cognitive and emotional ability to pass an in-person Turing test."

"Can I help train her? That way, I'll know what to expect from her and vice versa."

"Electra-C expects that."

Erika nodded knowingly before saying,

"It sounds like she told you a lot. Did she mention I'll be relocating to my new office in London?"

"Yes, and you'll arrange for your A-Team to shuttle you and Lily in early December."

Erika ended the Indy-M discussion and started walking away, but she stopped abruptly, then slapped her forehead and turned to Indy-M.

"I know you'll keep tabs on the Japanese company when it's constructing the Lily android. When it's ready to ship, why don't I have the A-Team deliver it?"

"Smart idea. When they tell me it's ready, I'll ask you for the delivery date."

"Perfecto Garcia, as they say in Mexico and Spain. Between now and my departure for London, I'll have plenty to do, so I'll start right now."

A curious thought flashed in Erika's brain while sauntering to her workstation.

Thanks to everything I've done the past couple of days, I'm feeling more relaxed, even though I have more to do for all my next moves.

I don't remember who told me about the Robert Frost poem

'Stopping by Woods on a Snowy Evening,' but I feel like the last verse is speaking to me;

The woods are lovely, dark, and deep.
But I have promises to keep,
And miles to go before I sleep,
And miles to go before I sleep.

I have one more conversation for today before I sleep. It's time to call the A-Team.

And it became the easiest of the day. When finished, they understood their two assignments: first, the Lily delivery, and then the pickup and delivery of Erika and Lily, which would include purchasing a suitable Glock pistol with an adequate supply of bullets, plus two magazines and a silencer. They told her to call several days ahead, and they would take care of the rest.

Satisfied when she ended the call, Erika knew it was time for sleep.

Chapter 4
November 2238

"Counting Down to the Departure"

Erika's to-do list for the move included meeting with Monet for Ambassador Project updates, reviewing current events in Washington, studying the White House press releases, and checking the European Union's reactions. It also included packing for the move and learning about both London's and England's history, plus their latest concerns. Finally, it included assisting Indy-M train Lily when the android arrived.

Erika had returned from a Washington meeting two days before the A-Team delivered Lily. Indy-M knew how to unpack the crate and begin training her, so Erika played the assistant's role.
After placing Lily on a wheel-mounted stretcher, Indy-M removed a set of manuals from the crate before speaking.
"These will tell us how to prepare and teach her. How does she look to you?"
"Like a real sleeping person. Her skin looks like the real thing. How do they do it?"
"Japanese engineers use cutting-edge materials and techniques to create skin that is difficult to distinguish from real human flesh. They call it frubber."
"Well, It sure fooled me. OK, how do we wake her up?"
"We charge the lithium batteries by plugging her into an electrical outlet. She'll come to life when they're fully charged."
Erika helped Indy-M push the stretcher into the assembly area and started reading while sitting. She did most of the reading because Indy-M had studied them online in the weeks preceding the delivery, which meant she could answer Erika's questions.
"Will she know where she is and who we are when she wakes up?"

"Yes. The Japanese company loaded software they call basal memory and a starting data set describing the Deus Lab and us. Her training will build on that."

"What will she do when she wakes up?"

"We will see when she does."

Erika read further before asking another question.

"It says we can adjust the muscular speed and strength before loading additional software. Do you know how to do that?"

"Electra-C has instructed me."

Erika thought for a moment before saying,

"Did she tell you to do some pre-training tests to compare with post-loading and training results?

"Yes."

"OK… I'm going for a Coke. I'll sit, sip, and be silent when I come back.

Lily woke up two hours later; they spent the rest of the day running pre-training tests before plugging her in for the night.

Indy-M summarized the results while Erika snacked in the dining area.

"She's stronger and quicker than you or me and speaks with a Cockney dialect. She passed the Turing test and answered questions about where she is."

Erika finished another Oreo before saying,

"How do you know about her accent?"

"The android company told me it's common in London."

"I like it. She speaks clearly and carries on a decent conversation while displaying some emotion. What's your guess for how she'll do after you make the muscular adjustments and load Indira's software?"

"She will do better physically, cognitively, and emotionally. How much better we won't know for certain until we test her again, but she should show improvement."

"OK, what time tomorrow will we continue?"

"You decide."

"OK, how about after I run and have a snack?"

"I will wait here until you return."

"Hey, I just thought of something. Can she wake up and unplug herself, or is plugging in a signal to wait for us to unplug her?"

"I don't know; we will have to ask…"

Erika's excitement woke her early and made her run half the usual distance, which meant Indy-M began making muscular adjustments at seven. Erika watched and talked only to herself.

I never paid attention until now to Indy M's logical and even-tempered personality; she's like a pre-test Lily. I'll do my informal comparison between post-test Lily and Indy-M but share what I find only with Electra-C.

Indy-M spent three hours making the muscular adjustments and 30 minutes more loading Indira's advanced software. Erika took a 30-minute workout and 10-minute snack break. Then, they did more testing, finally plugging her in at 7 p.m.

Indy-M spoke after Lily went to sleep.

"We can hold our pre versus post-test discussion now."

"No way. I'm going for a run to unwind. I'll find you when I get back…"

Sitting in the dining area two hours later, Erika nibbled on a peanut butter and banana sandwich while Indy-M talked.

"As expected, post-test Lily is stronger, faster, and more agile with the adjustments and software. She should be equal to our Robo-Soldiers, and they are superior to any your enemies might have. And her facial expressions show more emotion than before. How would you compare pre versus post-test speaking and thinking?"

"She carries on a smoother and more nuanced conversation, and her words and sentences sound almost as smart as me. Oops, I better correct that to as smart as mine. Do you think they'll get even better with more training?"

"We'll find out. Come get me tomorrow morning when you finish running. I will observe Lily through the night while you rest."

Each went their separate way, but instead of resting, Erika invoked Electra-C's avatar and spoke when she appeared.

"We now have Lily up and running. After Indy-M made the muscular adjustments and loaded Indira's advanced software, we did the pre-versus-post testing, which shows she's better than any android currently in production. She seems almost human. Is that what you expected?"

"Yes, but we are limited by Japanese android technology, which is the world's best. If the Deus Lab were equipped for android manufacturing, there would be no need to compare ours to the competition, because no mere mortal will ever match Indira."

"And what you just said segues to what I want to do. I'm in the mere mortal category, but Indy-M's beyond that. She can train Lily twenty-four-seven, but I can't, so please tell Indy-M to proceed without me. I'll do other things on my to-do list. That'll speed up the countdown to departure. And I don't want to see Lily again until Indy-M finishes the training. You wanna hear my reasoning?"

"Of course. Please continue."

"I'm using the 'raising a child' metaphor. What Indy-M's doing is a combination of giving birth to and raising Lily until she's ready to start her first job. That's where I come in. I'll be her on-the-job trainer. Whatacha think?"

Electra-C's expression became like that of a mother talking about her favorite child's latest accomplishment.

"I am proud of how you have grown after Terri's death. At the rate you are improving, you will soon be among the best."

Erika's gasp hinted at her surprise, but she recovered to say,

"I'm trying to prove I'm worthy of the Lightning Brain Legacy."

"Well, please carry on, as will I."

Electra-C vanished before she could see Erika's emerging smile appear after wiping away a tear or two.

More progress to come on the tasks I must do.

Erika attended an Ambassadors Project meeting in Washington the following week. Monet had invited the most influential Indian and African contacts. She also included those from the NAIA and IPWA.

Erika's incisive explanation of an Indian-African econo-political alliance convinced even the most skeptical. Afterward, when Monet invited her to a Thanksgiving dinner, Erika asked for a favor.

"I'd love to come, and I'd also like to spend more time in DC. Could I stay at your place the week before?"

"Certainly. You're a wonderful house guest. Call me the day before you plan to arrive."

"I will, and please thank Alonzo too…"

Upon returning to the Deus Lab, Erika chose another task from her to-do list that would be the most fun: learning about London and England's history. Because of her Web-surfing skills, she thought it would take little time, but that wasn't so. Her frustration showed when she gave the keyboard an open-palm slap.

There's too much information. How can a sift through it?… I got it… I'll ask the latest ChatGPT software to give me a summary. I'll do England first and then London. And I'll run it in written rather than spoken mode so l can print the report and study it whenever I have the time.

Twenty minutes later, she marveled at the printout.

Historical Summary of England

England's history spans thousands of years, marked by significant cultural, political, and social transformations.

Prehistoric and Roman England

- **Early Settlements**: Human habitation in England dates back over 800,000 years, with modern humans arriving during the Ice Age around 35,000 years ago. Evidence of early societies includes tools and structures such as Stonehenge.
- **Roman Conquest (43 AD)**: The Romans invaded under Emperor Claudius, establishing Roman Britain. They built roads and towns and introduced advanced governance. Rebellions like Boudicca's uprising (60 AD) occurred but were suppressed.

Anglo-Saxon and Viking Periods

- **Anglo-Saxon Era (5th–11th Century)**: Following the Roman withdrawal in the 5th century, Germanic tribes (Angles, Saxons, and Jutes) established kingdoms that shaped early English identity and introduced Old English.
- **Viking Invasions**: Starting in the late 8th century, Vikings raided and settled parts of England. The Danelaw was established in the northeast but was eventually subdued by Anglo-Saxon kings like Alfred the Great.

Norman Conquest and Medieval England

- **Norman Conquest (1066)**: William the Conqueror defeated Harold II at the Battle of Hastings, becoming King of England. The Normans introduced feudalism and reshaped governance and culture.
- **Middle Ages**: Marked by internal conflicts like the Wars of the Roses (1455–1487), economic growth through the wool trade, and religious shifts leading to Protestantism.

Tudor and Stuart Eras

- **Tudor Period (1485–1603)**: Under Henry VIII, England broke from the Catholic Church to form the Church of England. Elizabeth I's reign saw cultural flourishing and early colonial expansion.
- **Stuart Period (1603–1714)**: This era included the English Civil War (1642–1651), leading to a brief republican government under Oliver Cromwell. The monarchy was restored in 1660 but faced further challenges during the Glorious Revolution (1688).

Union with Scotland and the Industrial Revolution

- **Formation of Great Britain (1707)**: England united with Scotland to form Great Britain. The Industrial Revolution began in England in the late 18th century, transforming society and establishing Britain as a global power.

Modern Era

- **Empire and Decline**: By the 19th century, Britain ruled a vast empire. However, decolonization in the 20th century reduced its global influence.

- **World Wars**: England played a central role in both World Wars, which weakened its economy but reinforced its cultural legacy.
- **Post-Modern Era.** The "Perfect Storm (Techno-Plague Pandemic, Heightened Terrorism, and Harsh Governments) that struck the world late in the 20th century pushed the developed nations into the Post-Modern Era, where it remains today.
- Biotechnology has reduced but not eliminated the impact of viral plagues. Isilabad-led Terrorism still wages the centuries-old war between Christianity and Islam, and the friction between Democratic versus Authoritarian governments continues.
- Unforeseen political and global events that affect the world's alignment of nations impact all developed nations.

Historical Summary of London

The three-way distinction between city, town, and village dates back to the 14th century -- but before that, there was just a two-way distinction: a town was anything larger than a village. London is older than the word "city," so it held onto the old name, "London Town".

London's history spans nearly two millennia, beginning with its foundation by the Romans in AD 43. They established Londinium as a civilian settlement, which grew into a thriving center of commerce.

After the Roman withdrawal in the 5th century, the medieval period began with William the Conqueror.

The Tudor period (1485-1603) saw significant changes, including Henry VIII's break with Rome and the dissolution of the monasteries, which altered the city's landscape.

Under Elizabeth I, London flourished as a center of culture, with figures like Shakespeare contributing to its artistic legacy.

The Industrial Revolution (1760-1840) transformed London dramatically. The city experienced rapid growth, becoming the world's largest city by 1825. New factories, particularly in textiles, created jobs and spurred urbanization. However, this growth also led to overcrowding, pollution, and poor working conditions.

The 19th century saw further expansion and improvements, such as new roads and the London Underground, which began operations in 1863

In the 20th century, London faced significant challenges, including damage from World War II bombing. However, the city rebuilt and resumed growing as a global financial and cultural center.

But like all major cities around the globe, it suffered through the "Perfect Storm" and is still dealing with its aftermath.

London remains one of the world's most important cities, blending its rich history with modern innovations and a diverse, multicultural population.

This is a great way to sift through Big Data. Let's see what ChatGPT gives me for England's current global worries.

The report took less than half the time to produce than the previous one because Erika knew how to structure the prompt. She reviewed it five minutes later.

The United Kingdom's Current Concerns

The UK is concerned about several international political events and challenges:

Global Geopolitical Instability

The UK is facing an increasingly volatile global situation, with concerns about:

1. Skirmishes in the Middle East and the Baltic States.
2. China's assertive global agenda and threats of invading Taiwan.
3. The durability of America's commitment to European security.

Great Power Dynamics

The UK is working to navigate unpredictable great power dynamics, particularly:

1. Rising Sino-US tensions.
2. China's strategic choices in trade and security policy.

European Relations

Improving relations with the European Union is a priority for the UK, aiming to:

1. Offset the risk of reduced US engagement in Europe.
2. Fill post-Brexit policy gaps.

Global Governance and International Development

The UK is focused on reinvigorating its role in:

1. Global governance institutions.
2. International development efforts.

Economic and Trade Concerns

The UK is grappling with:

1. The potential rise of protectionism and further 'securitization' of trade.
2. The success of World Trade Organization reform.
3. Balancing economic security interests with support for the rules-based trading system.

Environmental and Health Challenges

The UK is preparing for potential destabilizing factors such as:

1. Environmental degradation and climate change.
2. Future pandemics.

Indo-Pacific Focus

The UK is implementing a 'tilt' towards the Indo-Pacific region, with a focus on:

1. Increasing national security protections against potential threats from China.
2. Engaging with the region through CPTPP trade agreements
3. Contributing to regional security through alliances and deployments

These concerns reflect the complex international landscape that the UK is navigating, balancing economic, security, and diplomatic interests in an increasingly uncertain global environment.

ChatGPT's becoming my best friend for data sifting and summary reporting. It'll help me launch GMS when I get to London, but I need a break to keep from winding up too much.

Erika's growing confidence showed in how quickly she breezed through the remaining tasks while she counted down to Thanksgiving. She collected all the documents and data sets needed for the London office setup. After that, she packed the minimal amount of items after deciding to buy a new set of clothes while settling in.

The night before Jason-M would drive her to Washington, Indy-M sat with her while she snacked. When she said she had finished packing, Indy-M said,

"I have completed all the Lily training I can do. It is time for you to meet her."

"OK, go get her."

Indy-M made the introductions several minutes later as Erika stood facing them.

"Lily Lloyd, this is Erika Kincaid. You are now her office manager and personal assistant."

Lily smiled demurely and extended her hand while saying,

"Hello, Ms. Kincaid. I will do my best for you."

Erika shook her hand before saying,

"Please call me Erika. According to Indy-M, you'll do on-the-job training with me. Do you know the basics for setting up an office?"

"Yes, Indy-M has been most thorough."

"Good, and I've done the same while counting down to our departure. People shake hands only when meeting for the first time, not again, even when saying goodbye, and in negotiations, know-it-all behavior and boasting are frowned upon – the UK is the land of elegant understatement."

"Right you are. Both of us will learn more once we arrive."

"You're right. I'll be back after spending Thanksgiving with my business partners in DC. I leave early tomorrow, so let's say goodbye."

Nodding before turning to leave, Lily seemed to know where to go. Before Indy-M turned to follow her, Erika said,

"Thanks to you, I think I've found my new best London friend."

"Yes, and she will make both of us proud…"

Erika used the days before Thanksgiving to meet with reporters and government contacts she had made from her journalism days working with Terri. She revealed no details of what she would be doing while collecting off-the-record comments about the turmoil roiling Washington.

When Monet insisted on preparing Thanksgiving dinner's main course, Alonzo volunteered to buy dessert, and Erika said she would buy the wine. She and Alonzo went shopping the night before while Monet started her preparations.

Watching the Macy's Thanksgiving Parade brought sudden sentimental sadness that she hid from Alonzo.

This could be the last time I watch it. I don't know what London holds… and I don't know how often I'll share personal time with Monet and Alonzo… come on, don't make yourself depressed… I've finished all London planning.

Erika's sadness departed, and everyone enjoyed the convivial atmosphere during dinner.

She kept the conversation light until dessert, when she gave Monet a summary of what she had learned from her meetings. When finished, Monet said,

"We know more than your contacts, but they think the White House will make a major announcement sometime in January. That's possible."

Erika said,

"And that's why I'm driving back tomorrow morning. I've done enough here to prepare for next year's projects. So have you, so why don't I call in January to push ahead on the Ambassadors Project?"

Alonzo looked ready to end the discussion.

"Well then, I propose a toast to Monet's Thanksgiving feast and our success for the coming year."

He poured more Champagne before leading the toast and helping the ladies clear the table.

Erika contacted the A-Team soon after returning to schedule pickup from the Deus Lab on Monday, and she used the entire weekend triple-checking everything.

Excitement kept her tossing and turning for an hour before finally falling into a fitful sleep, but she awoke in the throes of a panic attack close to 3 a.m.

Jeezus H. Christ, the countdown's at zero and the marathon's starting gun's about to fire. But can I get to the finish line? I gotta talk with Electra-C.

Erika dashed to a workstation to summon her and spoke immediately.

"I'm in the middle of a panic attack. Everything so far has been like practicing for the big race. It'll start when the A-Team gets here, but I won't have my partner Terri with me to share the load. Do you think I've done enough preparation for London?"

"Your London planning has been exceptional. At the time of Terri's unfortunate demise, she relied on you for planning, and your journalistic and people skills matched hers. And please consider this – Lily is your new partner. Indy-M has trained her for office management and bookkeeping, and she knows more about getting around in old London Town than you might ever.

"Keep her with you at all times so she gets to know you and vice versa. She'll become even more and more lifelike, the more she interacts with other people, and don't tell anyone she's an android; let them figure it out, and if they do, tell little."

Erika's heaving breathing subsided.

"You're right. I hadn't looked at it this way until right now. I'll try to go back to sleep."

"But before you do, please tell me your contingency plan."

Her puzzled look gave the answer before she said,

"For what?"

"If a situation arises that you and Lily can't handle, Lily knows to call Indy-M if you can't, and if the two of them can't get you out of whatever predicament you are in, Indy-M knows to call me. And in the unlikely event that the three of us can't retrieve you, I will call Indira. And if Indira and I cannot save you, humanity's world is coming to an end."

Erika took one deep breath and closed her eyes to settle herself while her sense of humor returned. Opening them, she said,

"The world doesn't need humans to keep spinning on its axis. I think you and Indira are here until the end of the ultimate marathon."

"Well put. Now go to bed and sleep until the A-Team arrives. And please remember, I am always watching from the Cyberspace shadows."

Electra-C vanished before Erika could say,

"Yes, Mother, I shall obey...."

Chapter 5
December 2238

"Settling In"

When the crew member assigned to help the two passengers saw Lily waking up, he unbuckled his seatbelt before leaning across the aisle to speak.

"You wake, partner, please. We're landing soon. I'm going to help the team." Then he exited the cabin, gripping the support bar as the plane descended.

Lily looked at Erika, who was asleep next to her in the seat window. Then she nudged her before saying,

"Ms. Erika, our flight's about to land. Please wake up."

Erika came to life, simultaneously stretching and groaning before saying,

"I'm stiff from sitting too long. You're lucky because that doesn't bother you, does it? Hey, how did you wake yourself up?"

"I have sensors that act like your nervous system. My battery sensor alerts me to recharge when running out of energy and wakes me when fully charged."

"And you can plug in wherever you find an outlet? I wish I could do the same. How long can you function before re-energizing? Wait, let me rephrase the question. How long can you stay awake before feeling like you need to sleep?"

"I have extra-strength batteries, which give me extra strength, speed, and endurance, and I have a backup system too, which is like your second wind. You will find I can keep pace with you."

"From the testing we did, your physical abilities are better than mine, and you might be smarter than me in some areas, thanks to Indy-M's training. I don't know the distance from Heathrow to downtown London. Do you?"

"It's twenty miles with a drive time of about an hour, no matter the time of day. The A-Team timed the flight so they could drop us at the Regis House by mid-morning."

"I bet you have plenty of memory capacity, too. I'll help you fill it up, and when we do, can we increase it?"

"Yes, but the technicians built me with so much that I doubt we can. You will find that the more information I store, the smarter I become, or as you like to say, the better my cognitive abilities seem."

Erika loosened her neck by rolling her head twice before saying more.

"There's a lot more for me to learn about you, and that'll happen as we work together, but how much did Indy-M teach you about me?"

"Indy-M told me as much as Electra-C felt useful. Why not discover how much in the months to come?"

"OK, but what about your emotions, or as Electra-C and I are fond of saying, your emotional persona?"

"It too will grow as I spend more time with people, so why not wait and see?"

"That'll work for me."

Erika didn't know what else to say, but a thought came to her when she leaned back. She tapped Lily on the arm and said,

"I'm glad the drive will take an hour. I'll use it to practice what I'll say to the building manager when we get there. After he shows us around, we'll unpack."

"How nice we each have only one suitcase. You also have your laptop and gun. How will you get it through security?"

"The A-Team put it in the concealed compartment of my laptop's shoulder bag, and they also gave us passports and I.D.s that show we're Londoners. And wherever we go, speak for yourself. I'll help if you need it. Do you feel ready to start?"

"Yes, and I'll help you with normal etiquette for both the business and personal worlds. Shall I drop the 'Ms' when it's just the two of us?"

"We're becoming close friends, so please do."

Erika felt the plane banking and the engines throttling back, prompting her to say,

"Check your seatbelt and get ready for our adventure to begin."

The helper returned minutes after the plane taxied to an unloading area.

"We get carry-ons off, then take you to hotel. You follow me, please."

Her stiffness still lingered when she and Lily reached their belongings, and when the team leader told them what they should do next, Erika spoke while twisting from side to side.

"No, just walk us out of this restricted area; we'll take a taxi to our hotel."

"Ho-Kay, you follow me, please."

Erika spoke only to herself as they trudged along, listening intermittently to Lily.

Even though I feel the penetrating dampness caused by the low-hanging gray clouds and their drizzle on my skin, they're not dampening my mood. I feel better with every step. Lily says London's December weather is usually chilly and wet, but it seldom snows; fog replaces it because of the stagnant air.

I'll let Lily talk to the cab stand guy. She says 'black cabs' is the proper term in London… and I'll pay with my business credit card that'll handle transactions in either dollars or pounds. Electra-C has thought of everything.

Once aboard, Erika said,

"You can be my tour guide in a couple of days, but I want to look out the window while thinking. Why don't you do the same?"

"That's the sensible thing to do, so I shall join you."

Both partners remained silent as they drove through neighborhoods and on tree-lined divided highways that were breadboard flat. Driving on the left didn't surprise her, nor did Londoners' slower speeds and more courteous behavior than American drivers.

By the time they reached downtown London, Erika stopped thinking about the office and began staring at the street scenes passing by.

The narrow streets and sidewalks look just like I see in the movies… lots of double-decker buses and black cabs. There's not as much foot traffic as I see in America's big cities… maybe the weather's the reason… and few people seem to rush about.

Lots of historic-looking stone buildings are spaced among modern, taller ones. I don't see many futuristic skyscrapers, but I'm not surprised. London's been here for over two thousand years. Living here is bound to be a colossal change of scenery.

When Erika identified herself at the building's security desk, the guard called the building manager. A dapper fellow who looked about Lily's age appeared several minutes later.

He extended his hand while saying,

"Good morning, Ms. Kincaid. My name is Oliver Newton. I'm pleased you arrived as planned."

"The planes and cabs got us here on time. This is my office manager, Lily Lloyd."

After greeting Lily the same way, he said,

"Follow me to my office where we'll make your building I.D.s, and then I will take you to your office."

Twenty minutes later, Oliver showed Erika how to open the office door with her I.D. and then whisked them around, explaining as they walked. When finished, he said,

"Your workstations, phone, and the telly in your living quarters are ready for you to use. So is the office area. We have stocked it with all the standard supplies. Your fridge is ready too, but you must stock it. Is there anything else I may assist with?"

"As a matter of fact, yes. Where can we go for more office supplies and get business cards, and where can we buy groceries?"

"There are several close by. Let me jot down the addresses. Would you like directions too?"

Lily said,

"No, thank you. I already know my way around the streets of London."

"From the way you speak, I thought you might. Very well, I shall leave you to have at it."

While he turned to leave, Erika said,

"Where's the fitness center, and will my I.D. get me in?"

"It is on the lower level, and your I.D.s will. Our fitness trainer works during the peak hours, which are five to seven in the morning and six to eight at night. Is there anything else?"

"No, sir. We are ready to go."

Erika and Lily visited the fitness center, stopping at a vending machine so Erika could buy some snacks and a Coke, which she gobbled before they hiked back to the office.

After unpacking their essential belongings, Erika said,

"I'll make a list of what we should buy," but Lily replied,

"No need to write it. Just tell me, and I will store it in memory."

"Good idea; OK, here it is…"

Lily showed her streets-of-London knowledge by leading them to the stores without backtracking once. She blended in with both pedestrians and people at the stores. and while buying groceries, she had a ready answer when Erika asked,

"Why don't they put the milk in refrigerated dairy cases?"

"Because Britain, like most of Europe, uses ultra-high pasteurization, which is like boiling, so it's safe at room temperature for months."

"How does it taste?"

"Why don't you try some when we return to the office?"

Erika tipped her head backward and blinked before leaning forward and saying,

"The more we talk, the more I hear your good ideas. Let's go."

Erika gave Lily her answer mid-afternoon while sitting at the office snack table, which was big enough for two.

"The milk's OK, but it's too bland if I don't sip it while eating something. And I think peanut butter and bananas taste the same no matter what country you're in. Hey, I've got another question for you. Can you sense things like sight, sound, taste, touch, and smell?"

"Yes, I have interconnected digital sensors embedded in my skin. It's like your nervous system. I already have sensation stimulus response stored from Big Data, and Indy-M's training added more, which you will do as we work together. I don't know how it works, but you should ask Electra-C."

Shrugging half-heartedly before taking one breath, Erika said,

"I'm beat, but I'll do it now. And I want the call to be private, so could you put yourself to sleep right now and wake up when I'm done?"

"Yes, and don't be alarmed by how I look. My nervous system will wake me at an appropriate time. Goodbye."

Lily froze like a sitting statue. Erika tidied the eating area before traipsing to her workstation. Appearing after a couple of keystrokes, Electra-C waited for Erika to speak.

"We've had quite a day settling in. We got to Heathrow fine and dandy, sight-saw by taking a cab, opened the office, and did some shopping. And I couldn't have done it without Lily. She's got sensors that make her seem human. How'd you and Indira do it?"

"You look tired, so I'll make it brief. We can talk philosophically about three personas – the physical, emotional, and cognitive – or describe people via the neuroscientific triune brain model that contains the reptilian brain for physical survival, the limbic system for feelings, and the neocortex for speech, logic, and higher thinking skills.

"Either way, Lily's sensors interconnect to three sets of computer chips loaded with Indira's software that mimic these personas. That's why she can move, show facial emotions, and when talking, seem to think.

"And if she seems human to you, just treat her like one. Let your perception be reality. If you do that, she will learn even better to be like one. Why don't you sleep on it?"

Erika's tired-looking eyes became brighter.

"Thank you for the reminders. I'll follow your advice when I wake up."

"Excellent, now rest easy."

When Erika opened her eyes, she saw Lily standing next to the bed. She sat up and said,

"Electra-C says if I think you're human, that's all that matters for taking our relationship to the next level, so when I pop out of bed, please let me hug you."

"Why yes, luv, please do…"

Chapter 6
December 2238

"Out and About"

Erika and Lily used the next week to prepare for their GMS launch campaign starting in January to get clients, targeting Britain first and then branching out to EU members. When Erika's creativity proved better than Lily's, Erika outlined the launch strategy, but Lily's superior memory came to the fore for other tasks. Erika assigned her two: Lily would flesh out the strategy and then structure its implementation steps.

When Erika saw they had completed everything on Monday the week before Christmas, she told Lily that evening what she planned for tomorrow.

"It's time we get out and about to do some networking. We'll visit the newsrooms of my former employers. We'll chat with Fraser Newton at IBN early tomorrow, followed by people I know at the New York Times. Whatcha think?"

"They are close by, so no matter the weather, I can walk us there. Have you called for an appointment?"

"No, it'll be better if we drop in unannounced."

"What are your intentions?"

"We'll find out what they think about the uproar in Washington. Then we'll ask for an intro to their closest circle of reporter friends who can add to our launch campaign target list."

"Well, it's time for you to rest. I will too, and I will wake you at 5 a.m. so you can exercise before we leave. Are we copacetic?"

"Yes indeed, so goodnight."

Lily froze into her sitting-statue pose; Erika went to bed.

As luck would have it, Erika spotted Fraser chatting with two office mates when they entered. As Erika led Lily toward him, he nearly dropped his coffee mug when recognizing her while turning to greet them.

"Why, it's Erika Kincaid. Welcome to London. Does this mean you found a job here?"

"Yes, and this is our office manager, Lily Lloyd."

After shaking hands, he said,

"How did you get past the security guard?"

"She recognized me from past visits."

"Very good. Working in London will be a pleasant change from the reporter's nightmare that's occurring in Washington. It's safer here. Reporters aren't thrown out of press conferences."

"DC's not a happy place these days. What do you make of the announced U.S.-Russian Alliance?"

"We're worried about the consequences of transitioning from a three to a two-superpower world. We've asked at press conferences what our government pundits think might happen, but they say it's too soon to speculate. But everyone agrees the White House will come out with a lightning bolt of a press release in January. What do you think?"

"My DC sources agree, and they think it'll include some bombshells. Here's one – the U.S. will withdraw from NATO."

"That's certainly a bolt from the blue. Any others?"

"I should have more when I let them know I've settled in. And I'll tell the next time we get together what they say."

"That gives me an idea. Why don't you come to the New Year's Eve party sponsored by the London chapter of the NUJ."

"What's that?"

"Lily's a Brit, isn't she? She certainly sounds like one. Let her tell us."

"It's the National Union of Journalists."

"Right you are. Have Lily call me if you can come, and I'll tell her when and where to go."

Fraser looked ready to end the conversation, so Erikas said,

"May I bring Lily?"

"The more the merrier."

Lily smiled pertly, then said,

"Thank you, Mr. Nelson. If you tell me the details, I'll remember."

After he did, Erika said,

"We'll see you on New Year's Eve, and I'll try to bring some good news."

Erika had much the same luck in the New York Times newsroom. She learned nothing new regarding the UK government's concerns about Washington, but did hand out business cards. When getting ready to leave, a reporter standing in the background brought out an emotion that made Erika wince.

She reminds me of Terri, my beautiful ex-partner. I have to talk to her.

When Erika approached, the reporter spoke first.

"I never saw you in person because I started working here long after you left, but my mates still tell tales about you and Terri Tarrant having the knack of winding'em up just for good sport. I'm Chelsea Clarke."

Erika shook her hand before saying,

"I enjoyed my time at the Times. Is this your first newspaper job?"

"Yes, and it's the bees' knees. I hope my career moves up like yours. You look only a couple of years older than me."

"I'm sure it will. Just keep learning and networking. Are you going to NUJ's New Year's Eve party?"

"I didn't get an invite, and it cheeses me off because I'm only a junior reporter."

Erika sensed Chelsea's embarrassment when she said nothing else, so she filled the void.

"Well, maybe we can do something about that. Let's swap cards and talk in January…"

Checking her cell phone while she and Lily walked back to the office, Erika noticed the noon hour approaching, and she wanted to go to a particular type of place, so she asked Lily,

"What's the best UK fast-food chain?"

"Why, that would be Greggs."

"Is there one we can walk to?"

"Why, yes, and you look happy. Are we celebrating how well the meetings went?"

"You bet. When we get there, you can order for me."

By the time they were next in line, the brisk walk calmed Erika and piqued her appetite. Lily said,

"I'll order the Ploughmans Oval Bite. It's a hearty sandwich that combines the classic flavors of a traditional Ploughman's platter in a convenient, bite-sized sandwich."

"What's on it?"

"It's a British pub staple, typically featuring crusty bread, cheddar cheese, pickled onions, butter, and relishes, with optional additions like hard-boiled eggs, cold meats, or pâté.

"I'll also order a triple-chocolate cookie and a bottle of Karma Cola, which offers a more ethical alternative to mainstream colas. It uses natural ingredients and has a distinct flavor profile."

"What's it tastes like?"

"You can tell me soon enough, luv."

Erika spoke after taking a couple of bites.

"The platter's pretty much like deli sandwiches I've had elsewhere, but the relish tastes like a blend of sugar and spices. What's it called?"

"Chutney, and it's made from a blend of fruits and vegetables seasoned with vinegar and sugar."

Lily watched while Erika finished the sandwich before sampling the cookie.

"It's fresher than I've had before. The soft texture makes it seem richer. Now, to the Karma Cola."

Erika's look showed pleasure after taking a couple of sips.

"Hey, I like its more subtle flavor and less carbonation than traditional soft drinks. Why the name, and does it contain caffeine?"

"Kola nuts provide an earthy flavor balanced by organic sugar, and although they contain caffeine, it is extracted during the manufacturing process."

"Is that the same type of nut used to make Coca-Cola?"

"Yes, but it also contains an extract from the cocoa bean that imparts a chocolate flavor and contains associated phytochemicals that help the plant resist fungi, bacteria, and viruses while keeping insects away."

Erika placed the bottle on the table before saying,

"From now on, I'll take all your dining recommendations…"

Having all the projects ready for the new year, Erika enjoyed working at a leisurely pace, which continued until Friday, four days away from Christmas. That's when Lily made another recommendation.

"I know how to navigate the London Underground, which is called the Tube because of its shape. But you should, too. Why don't we ride it tomorrow?"

"Good idea. Can I see a map before we do?"

"Of course. I'll print one and an article I'll use to explain it."

Erika skimmed them before Lily started talking.

"It's one of the oldest metro systems in the world, opening in 1863. This comprehensive network serves Greater London, comprising eleven rail lines, almost 250 miles in length, and numbering 272 stations. It is divided into nine travel zones, with Zone 1 covering central London and zones 6 to 9 extending to the outskirts. And it's plenty deep. Londoners survived the World War Two blitz by sheltering in the stations."

Erika waved the hand not holding the printouts before saying,

"I've heard enough. That's plenty until tomorrow…"

The two spent most of the day exploring the Tube system with its bright lighting, well-kept stations, and clean, on-time trains, but late Saturday afternoon, when pulling into Victoria Station. Lily hurried them off, explaining after the train pulled out.

"We are close to the West End Theater District, and tonight would be ideal for absorbing its charm by walking around."

Erika's painful expression came with her words.

"You're not, but I'm certainly hungry. You'd better pick a place to snack."

"I know what you might like – Ben's Fish and Chips. We'll get a place to sit because the restaurants fill up after the shows let out, not before."

The pair blended in with the happy throng, enjoying their position on its fringe. Suspended in the eerily empty glow of the lights illuminating now-deserted streets, they hiked back to the station after the crowds had dispersed into the theaters.

The platform had much the same atmosphere, so they waited in silence, recapping privately the day's adventure, but that changed abruptly when two twenty-something toughs approached obliquely. When closed, one snatched Erika's shoulder bag before galloping past. Second, wielding a knife. followed, but they made a mistake when stopping five yards away to taunt the victims. They never had a chance to hurl insults.

Lily charged toward the knife holder, tackling and crashing him onto the concrete before grabbing his knife and going after the bag holder, who dropped it and fled for the exits.

Erika was still gaping when Lily handed her the bag and said,

"They'll think twice before attacking seemingly defenseless females again."

"Hu-how did you know what to do?"

"I learned from Indy-M many skills that will be useful."

"Can you tell me some others?"

Hearing their train approaching, Lily said,

"I can do that another time, or better still, demonstrate when it's needed. You have seen and done enough for one day, so let's go home…"

Lily had other recommendations, which she gave on Sunday morning.

"You should take in the splendor of a Christmas Eve Midnight Service at Saint Paul's Cathedral. The boys' choir and celebrity scripture readers perform with typical British aplomb. Then on Christmas Day, after you go for a run along the Thames, we'll have Christmas Day Dinner at the Park Plaza's Westminster Buffet that will fortify you for London's post-Christmas Boxing Day, which is December 26th. Stores run shopping deals, similar to America's Black Friday, and fans cheer on traditional sporting events such as soccer, cricket, rugby, horse racing, and even hunting."

"That'll let us replenish our wardrobe, and let's buy something to make a statement at the New Year's Eve party."

The results of each recommendation are added to the following: The pristine ambience of the Christmas Eve Service triggered Erika's hopes for a better world and added to their enjoyment of the sumptuous buffet. When a waiter asked why Lily wasn't eating, she said,

"I'm trying to lose a few pounds, so I'm just taking in the wonderful aromas." Satisfied, the bloke poured more water and went on his merry way.

When Lily led the way to the always popular December 26th Boxing Day department store sales at Westfield Stratford City, Erika bought enough outfits to have the items delivered rather than lugging them around. All that remained was the New Year's Eve party, for which Erika and Lily looked ready to network for new business.

Spotting Fraser, Erika ambled toward him with Lily right behind. He turned to greet her when she stopped close by.

"What ho; hey, everyone, here's our American colleague I was telling you about, Erika Kincaid. She's just opened the London office for a consulting business. Goodness, what a snappy outfit she's wearing. Let's hear if what she's predicting for the New Year's political scene looks as good."

Erika paused for effect while handing out business cards to those now clustered about her, then spoke.

"With me is my office manager, Lily Lloyd. The name's Global Monitoring Services, or GMS for short."

She paused again, this time for Fraser.

"Erika combines investigative reporting with a selection of impressive forecasting apps, she prompts with questions her clients ask. Say again what you think will happen early January in Washington."

"Watch and listen for disruptive announcements from the U.S.-Russian Alliance. The United States will announce its withdrawal from NATO, and Russia will get a seat in the Guardian Party president's cabinet from which to direct foreign policy."

Her predictions stunned the audience for only a moment before people started chiming in.

"Impossible… too big of a shock… the EU won't stand for it…"

Erika timed her next predictions to build on what she had just said.

"Sorry, but there's more. The U.S. will slap selective tariffs on vaccine exports to countries that criticize the Alliance, and it will expel foreign reporters and bar from press conferences domestic ones who are critical of the Alliance."

Erika noticed a group forming around a fellow whom Fraser introduced.

"Clive Milton of the London Times always has a novel point of view. Let's hear his take on the Alliance."

"Erika's predictions are sobering and illustrate how inundating its people or other nations with its revolutionary proposals might paralyze them, but the EU can't sit on the sidelines. And think about this—the Alliance poses an even more menacing threat that falls within the purview of 'Surveillance Capitalism.' Would anyone care to give a working definition of what that is?"

No one did; Erika spoke only to herself.

This dark-haired guy looks handsome and smart. I don't know what he's talking about, so I better listen.

Clive had everyone's undivided attention while explaining.

"Surveillance Capitalism is the brainchild of Shoshana Zuboff, spelled out in her doorstop of a book 'The Age of Surveillance Capitalism, subtitled the Fight for a Human Future at the New Frontier of Power.' It's the unilateral claim by the giant digital companies that private human experience is a free raw material for them to translate into behavioral data. These data are then digitized and packaged into prediction products sold into the behavioral futures markets — business customers with a commercial interest in knowing what we consumers will do now, soon, and later.

"And here's what's terrifying. The U.S.-Russian Alliance controls world-leading Cyberspace Counter-Terrorism software. U.S. policy used to use it to keep QAnon and other Terrorgram-like militant, trans-national, radicalization, or blogging sites and chat room networks from getting out of control.

"The FBI and CIA have SWAT teams that are supposed to go after them, but the new Alliance promotes these blogging sites and chat room networks that spread fake news, so these SWAT teams might be instructed to let them be. If that happens, fake news could run rampant, making it hard for average blokes to know the truth about what's really going on, and those who get radicalized by lies often go out to kill the innocent before killing themselves afterward and becoming saints and heroes, furthering disrupting an already sorry state of affairs. This is transnational terrorism. I hope I'm being an alarmist, but the New Year could be problematic at best."

Although Clive's words had a depressing effect on everyone within earshot, Erika fought back.

"Please remember that we, the people, collectively determine the future, so let's try to be optimistic. And if you hire me, we can consider future scenarios."

Clive ended the discussion by saying,

"If Washington roils the climate in January, I might be your first client. We'll have to wait and see what DC says. But let's drink a toast to better days ahead..."

Chapter 7
January 2239

"Lightning Strikes Old London Town"

The White House didn't wait for New Year's Eve hangovers to lift before blasting a series of press releases onto a shocked world, for which Erika took little satisfaction getting right. She also guessed the identity of the person who called that evening.

"Hello, Clive. DC fired its lightning bolt of an announcement sooner rather than later, which gives the press its marching orders. Where do you plan to start?"

"By being your first London client. How about meeting at my office in the News Building first thing tomorrow morning?"

"I know where your newsroom is. Please tell the security guards you're expecting me and Lily."

"Roger that; see you then."

Lily and Erika arrived simultaneously with Clive, which gave them immediate passage through the security station and access to the newsroom via the lift. Erika made coffee after retrieving a Coke from the fridge while he dished up a plate of a Londoner's favorite breakfast treat—oatcakes with maple syrup—and explained his intentions.

"I want to interview typical Londoners to report their reactions to what your forecasting app makes of my prompt, which will have two parts and go something like this: the United States and Russia have developed subsea technology for mining huge, recently discovered Antarctic mineral deposits. How will the international community react if they make it the fifty-first state? And how might this affect rare earths exports to other countries needed for advanced AI chip fabrication?"

"I hadn't heard about their mining breakthrough, but the U.S. has been angling since the mid-18th century to purchase

Greenland from Denmark for reasons of national security, but the people of both Greenland and Denmark continue to oppose it."

"Right you are, but Antarctica is different. No people other than researchers live there, and no country has ever laid claim to it. It is governed internationally under the Antarctic Treaty, signed on December 1, 1959. This treaty ensures Antarctica is used only for peace and scientific research."

"Maybe so for right now, but the U.S.-Russian Alliance has gobs of economic, technological, and military power that'll disrupt the international balance of power. There's much more to consider, but we'll save that for later. For the time being, I'll wordsmith your prompt and give you my best forecast."

"You want to do that here or at your office?"

"I work better at mine. I'll call you when I have it done…"

Erika invoked Electra-C's avatar once she and Lily arrived at the office to produce Clive's report. Two minutes later, Erika retrieved the forecast from her printer and studied it before asking questions.

Socio-Political Forecast for the London Times Prompt

- **Expect the U.S.-Russian Alliance to push its subsea mining technology superiority if the other nations don't pool their resources to oppose it.**
- **The same applies to claiming the Antarctic as its 51st state.**
- **The Alliance needs a new source of rare earths to replace those on American Indian Reservation land.**
- **Expect the Alliance to push for all three within the next twelve months.**

"You think the world community is going to let the Alliance bully them?"

"Not if your Ambassadors Project gains traction. An Indian African Superpower aligned with China and the European Union could keep it in line, but much depends on the zeitgeist of the American people. The stories are not yet told."

"Well, thanks to you, Clive will have a shocking story to tell his interviewees. I'll send this to him right now."

Erika let Clive lead the conversation when he called two hours later.

"I say, this is jolly good stuff. It looks like the Alliance is thumbing its nose at the benefits of globalization and international trade. The result might be the loss of jobs and an increase in prices for most Americans."

"When you combine this report with selective tariffs the U.S. is slapping on vaccine exports, ask your political pundits how quickly the EU will strengthen its commitment to international trade and be willing to use military force to oppose what the Alliance is doing."

"I'll also ask Londoners what they think. And while I'm doing this, what will you do?"

"I'll go back to Washington and push ahead on other projects. I'll call you when I get back, which should be no later than early February, and by then, I'm sure you'll be ready for me to run another prompt."

"Right-oh. Be safe…"

Erika avoided potential airline disruptions by having the A-Team shuttle her and Lily back to the Deus Lab, where she prepared for a meeting that would be held at Monet's Zimbabwean embassy office in Washington first thing on Wednesday, January 9th. This time, she let Lily drive but kept her in the car.

Monet had invited the right people from those nations and organizations already committed to the Ambassadors Project, for which the Indian-African Alliance would be the centerpiece. When everyone agreed that this new alliance should issue a press release to counter the confusion coming from the White House, Monet ended the meeting by saying,

"I'll have Erika draft it and send you copies before it hits the news wires."

When someone asked when that would be, Erika said,

"You'll have it no later than next Monday, and the world will soon know we're not going to let the U.S.-Russian Alliance push us around."

Monet met privately with Erika afterward.

"Please let me approve it before you send it, and the next time we meet, be ready to discuss how we can fight back."

"Will do, and I'm leaving immediately to start on it." Erika focused on it during the drive back.

Though it was dark by the time Lily parked near the Deus Lab entrance, Erika took an abbreviated workout to remove the stress and stiffness from thinking and sitting too long. Then she showered and changed into leisure clothes before talking with Lily while snacking at her workstation.

"I'll finish the press release without anyone's help, but I'll get Electra-C's opinion before I send it to Monet. That way, I'm certain she'll approve it, and when she does, I'll tell her I'll send it on Monday, but I won't tell her I'll send advance copies to Clive and Chelsea. Can you guess why I'm doing that?"

"I can think of several reasons. It will strengthen your relationship with each other, and that will allow you to learn more from Clive and feel good by helping Chelsea while she helps you relive some of the emotions you shared with Terri."

"Hey, you're beginning to know better than anyone except Electra-C how I think and feel."

Lili replied,

"And I hope it's mutual."

Erika stretched while sitting before saying,

"Me too. Now, please let me be while I write…"

Using a familiar press release template, she reviewed her handiwork three hours later.

FOR IMMEDIATE PRESS RELEASE (PUT IN THE DATE)
Contact Person
Company
PREFERRED PHONE NUMBER
PREFERRED WEBSITE

THIS JUST IN: INDIA AND AFRICA ANNOUNCE THE NEXT SUPERPOWER ALLIANCE

Company Location: Person from Company has just learned from a confidential source that a daring Indian-African Alliance, led jointly by India and a coalition of African nations represented by Zimbabwe, has been officially launched to implement two primary goals:
BECOME THE NEXT SUPERPOWER AND OPPOSE THE GLOBAL AMBITIONS OF THE U.S.-RUSSIAN ALLIANCE.

Person from Company had more to say. "India and African nations share the strengths implicit in large, growing, democratic-leaning populations, and possess others that are complementary. This alliance will become the next Superpower, giving the world a better choice than the U.S.-Russian Alliance or China."

Recent White House announcements cast doubt on its suitability for leading the Free World. Indigenous people around the globe recognize this. In particular, the Native American Indian (NAIA) and the Indigenous Peoples Worldwide Alliance (IPWA) have already expressed their support. Others will too once they discover how this new Superpower can rein in growing threats from the U.S.-Russian Alliance.

Person concludes with this final observation. "The new Superpower has plans underway to bolster its 3-D and Cyberspace defenses. And that means it will soon have the muscle to deter aggression. Look for additional details as they become available."

About The Company
Give a paragraph description of the Company.
###

Satisfied, she contacted Electra-C, who spoke immediately.

"Monet will like the tone and content, and your sending it ahead to your London reporters will add credibility. But have you thought about what muscle the new Superpower needs?"

"Uh, no, but I thought you might help me there."

"I already have, but find out what Clive thinks before I give you more."

"OK, and that means I'd better return to London before Monday. How does that sound?"

"Almost as good as the press release. Now go make it happen."

Chapter 8
January 2239

"Washington Warnings"

The A-Team shuttled Erika and Lily back to London without incident, which meant Erika had settled in and decompressed enough to call Clive Saturday morning, reminding herself to practice enough British etiquette and diplomacy before segueing to what she wanted.

"I'd like to give you a press release before I send it to everyone else. If that's of interest, why don't you come to my office for all the details?"

"Why yes, what time works for you?"

"I know you're smart, but the sooner the better because you'll need all the time to get ready between our meeting and Monday when I release it."

"Well, why don't I arrive by ten and bring sandwiches and biscuits so we can work through the midday meal?"

"You call'em biscuits, but I call'em cookies. Either name works, and I'll supply the Karma Cola. See you soon."

After unlocking the entry door, when she heard tapping, Lily greeted the fellow when he entered.

"Hello, Mr. Milton. How nice you are so punctual. Erika is expecting you. If you would like a cup of coffee, we'll stop in the snack area before I take you to her office."

"Why, thank you, and if you would be so good, please pop our lunches into the fridge. I brought one for you, too."

"How thoughtful. Thank you. Now, please follow me."

Erika rose to greet Clive several minutes later, before pointing to the chair on the other side of her desk. He sipped his coffee as Erika began talking after they sat.

"I'm sending a press release for a client that's bound to send shock waves through the international community. Please study it before I tell you more." Erika slid a copy across the desk, then glanced nervously at hers while waiting for him to finish.

He looked at her five minutes later and said,

"I commend your work. It has the form and content written by a crackerjack journalist. Anyone you send it to will know what it means, why it's important, and where to put in their information before sending it on its merry way. So, what would you like me to do?"

"At the very least, you should be aware in case someone reports it before you, but why not have the London Times be the first?"

Clive sat up and rubbed his chin before saying,

"I could do that, but it will be more impactful if I write an editorial published later in the week that delves into the ramifications. Or are you planning to do that?"

"I wish I could, but you've got more brains and background to do that better than I. Uh, let me correct my grammar—better than I."

"Maybe not. There's a lot here, but I'll take a crack at it. How about I show it to you before it goes to press?"

"This is even better than I had hoped. Perhaps you could explain your approach, and I could chip in between now and lunch if I have something to offer. Maybe that'll help get you started."

"Well then, let's do so…"

Erika did most of the listening for the next two hours, but she did manage to contribute some ideas that Clive liked, and both needed a break by the time Lily brought in lunch. Afterward, they worked for another hour before Clive said he should be on his way and promised to show her his final copy. Erika thanked him but said she'll see it when it comes out in the London Times. Soon after he left, Erika shared her excitement with Lily.

"Clive's one sharp Brit. He's gonna write an editorial that'll come out later in the week and will build on my press release and the problems emerging in Washington. I'm so keyed up from what he told me, I'm gonna go for a run to unwind."

"I know how much the endorphin rush from running helps you think about things. Perhaps you can decide what role Chelsea can play for your press release rollout."

"Gads, I completely forgot. Thanks for reminding me. Maybe I'll come back with an answer…" Ninety minutes later, she told Lily.

"When I meet Chelsea for lunch tomorrow, I'll give her a copy of the press release and tell her to share it with her New York Times boss. They can decide how to scoop the U.S. media by reporting it first."

Lily's calm voice echoed her reassuring words.

"I'm sure Chelsea will find a way to return your kindness."

Erika waved when she spotted Chelsea sitting in a booth at a popular casual-dining place convenient for both, and she wasted no time getting to the point. After sitting down, she handed her a copy of the press release and spoke immediately.

"It won't release what I'm giving you until tomorrow. I wrote it for an important client, and you can beat the competition if you and your boss put it in the New York Times or on a broadcast before any other U.S. newspaper. What it says about the Indian African Alliance is clear, but practice what you'll say to your boss so he buys in."

Erika waited for Chelsea's look of surprise to change to one of gratitude before asking,

"Why are you doing this?"

"You remind me of my dearly departed partner, Terri Tarrant. Terri helped me early in my career, and I would like to help you."

Chelsea reached across with both hands, and when Erika grasped them, said,

"Thank you. I know we'll become great friends."

"I do too; hey, here comes the waitress; let's celebrate by ordering something to fit the occasion…"

Upon returning to the office, Erika shared the news with Lily, who said,

"You're making wonderful progress in old London Town, building the business and a network of friends."

"You better change you're to we're. I couldn't do it without you."

Lily didn't need to say a word. Erika could read them in her smile.

Erika felt so confident about what she had just put in place that she decided not to talk with Electra-C until after it unfolded. She liked the tone and timing of the New York Times' early Monday broadcast, and she rushed to the newsstand to check every edition of the London Times for Clive's editorial, which came out in Thursday morning's early edition.

She studied it for an hour before calling Clive.

Washington Warnings:
The American People Deserve Better
by Clive Milton, The London Times Senior Journalist/Editorialist

I imagine most people have read or heard about the just-announced Indian African Alliance, as summarized in its press release. There are many ramifications, especially when factoring in current and future disruptions to the world community caused by the U.S.-Russian Alliance. Hence, the title of this editorial.

My studies in history and politics, combined with my working experience, have shown that America's government and culture, though deeply flawed, are nonetheless powerful forces for good on the world stage, thanks to the character and can-do spirit of the American People. America used to embody a grand, heroic partnership between the government and its people locally, and a grand, heroic one between the United States and other nations internationally.

But no longer. What is emerging from the U.S.-Russian Alliance resembles George Orwell's dystopian novel "1984." It shows what can happen when a government and its elite supporters seek power without any morals or vision of the good. The U.S.-Russian Alliance may indeed signal that the U.S. government is entering a period of anti-democratic, power-seeking leaders.

American political historians say this has happened in the past: Democratic President Andrew Jackson in the 1830s, several Republican presidents in the 2010s and 20s, and Guardian Party President Jarred Gardner in the 2090s. In these cases, the United States reached a point of traumatic disruption, and the People took back the power that is rightfully theirs. How did they do it?

- By shifting their values back to Diversity, Equity, and Individuality, which leads to reduced economic and social inequality.
- By sticking together through the tough times, which leads to a strong national identity.
- By declaring a civic renaissance, leading to a national reassessment and political reform.
- By expanding the economy which all social and economic classes gain.

But might conditions be different this time? Consider this: the world order is beginning to transition from a three-superpower World (The United States, China, and Russia) to one that has only two (the U.S.-Russian Alliance, and China), and both of them are more authoritarian rather than democratic, don't trust their People, and don't want government or social institutions (courts and religions) reining in their power via checks and balances.

The three-superpower World we used to have demonstrated how three superpowers could stabilize international politics even though each followed its own goals. There's an analogy I would like to make that comes from physics, which is the Three-Body Problem:

- It is the statement that if you have three bodies gravitating toward each other under Newton's law of gravitation, there is no general closed-form solution for that situation. Little differences get amplified and can lead to wildly unpredictable future behavior.

Perhaps this is the overarching reason why the World needs to support the Indian African Alliance.

She didn't give Clive a chance to say a word after he said hello.

"This is Erika. I've been reading your editorial over and over for the past hour. It's brilliant. I hope I can work with you to build on what's in it."

"Why, thank you. I would like that. Why don't you call me next week after I hear how people in my network have reacted to it?"

"That'll work, and while you're doing that, I'll start listing what we might do."

"I will, too. Bye for now."

When the call ended, Erika told Lily what she would do.

"I'm gonna go for another run, and when I get back, I'll call Electra-C."

"And I'll have some biscuits and Karma Cola waiting for you when you do."

And even though the weather that morning was much brighter than Clive's editorial, Erika's excitement made her ready for whatever might be coming her way.

Chapter 9
January 2239

"Nets and Networks"

Erika had rehearsed during the run what she would say when invoking Electra-C's avatar that afternoon, which she did after eating the snack Lily had put on the table. Electra-C listened patiently for ten minutes, and when Erika said,

"So, that's where I'm at. Whatcha think?" Electra-C took over.

"Clive's editorial did a masterful job alerting the international community to upcoming problems deliberately incited by the U.S.-Russian Alliance. Both you and he will talk with your contact networks to assess what other nations think, but none of them will know the breadth and depth of what I have prepared for you."

When Electra-C stopped talking and the printer started whirring, Erika sat still until it stopped. Then, she retrieved the document and studied it while saying nothing, knowing that Electra-C would continue soon.

Dangerous Conflicts Coming
The International Community versus the U.S.-Russian Alliance

An undeclared war has already begun between those two combatants. They are battling for dominance over these Resources:
Energy:
- **China is the world leader in renewable energy (wind, solar, geothermal, and ocean currents.**
- **Green energy includes nuclear power, hydropower, and biomass.**
- **Brazil, Argentina, and U.S. are the world leaders in biomass energy. It is called green because it doesn't damage the environment.**

- **The U.S.-Russian Alliance will push for fossil fuels and nuclear energy because its energy companies and infrastructure are geared for it.**
- **The rest of the world will push for renewable and green energy.**
- **China will use its wind and solar technology to fight U.S.-Russian Alliance vaccine tariffs.**
- **Hydrogen power is not in the mix for this book!**

Rare Earths:
- **The U.S.-Russian Alliance and China will battle for rare earths for computer chip manufacturing.**

Vaccines:
- **U.S.-Russian Alliance will use its biotech superiority to bully the world**

Food:
- **U.S.-Russian Alliance will use U.S. farming to bully the world. Russia will violate the law of the sea fishing restrictions.**

Minerals:
- **U.S.-Russian Alliance will use its subsea mining technology to get what it wants.**

Global Warming and Climate Change:
- **Global Warming threatens rising sea levels, which threatens the rest of the world more than the U.S.-Russian Alliance.**
- **Climate Change (severe weather, droughts, floods) threatens all countries equally.**

Air and Water:
- **Everyone is affected in the same way by air. U.S.-Russia is better positioned for freshwater.**

Electra-C did so ten minutes later.

"Share these bullet points with no one. Use them when needed to contribute to what Clive or Monet says. I have details for each bullet point and others too, but I will reveal them when appropriate."

Erika's frown showed her confidence had begun shifting to concern when she said,

"I think I know how to use this with Clive, but what about Monet?"

"Indira and I want you to explain to her that the United States needs a new political party committed to the Indian African Alliance for the reasons summarized in Clive's editorial. The existing four are merely minions of the U.S.-Russian Alliance.

"Indira has chosen its name—the Matriarchate Party. It supports democratic and traditional American values, DEI initiatives blended with Meritocracy, and a dedication to Isocracy, a form of government invented by ancient Greek philosophers where all citizens have equal political power."

Electra-C waited for Erika's questions she saw forming.

"What does Matriarchate mean, and who's going to join?"

"Matriarchate is an adjective derived from the noun Matriarchy, which is a social system in which women hold all the positions of power and privilege. In a broader sense, it can also extend to moral authority, social privilege, and control of property.

"Once you convince Monet, she will covertly recruit seasoned congresswomen to champion its development. Once momentum starts building, they might recruit some congressmen to join. Your role is to assist Monet."

Erika's look shifted back to one of confidence.

"I'm beginning to see how all the pieces fit. I'll meet Clive first, and after that, I'll hold one with Monet."

"Excellent. I shall leave you to proceed. Don't wait for Clive to contact you. Set up a meeting with him and contact me afterward."

Electra-C vanished. Erika went for some chocolates and a Karma Cola.

Erika did enough preparation over the weekend to call Clive Monday morning, but Chelsea's call surprised her before she could.

"Guess what? My boss liked what we did with your press release and is thinking about the London office of the New York Times becoming another one of your clients. When could you meet with him and me at our office?"

"Let's see, you're in the News Building, aren't you?"

"That's right, and we're both here now."

"It's an easy walk for me and Lily. How about nine-thirty?"

"Perfect. See you then."

The brisk walk gave Erika all the time she needed to rehearse what she would say, while reminding herself to let Chelsea's boss lead the conversation. He started when she and Lily were seated opposite him and Chelsea at a table in a sleek-looking conference room.

"Giving Chelsea your press release before releasing it to the media was a win-win-win. It showed me Chelsea's got talent, it impressed our home office, and it might get you another client. Tell me how you work with them."

"It's standard. You hired me on an annual basis, and I picked one of your reporters to be my primary contact, which would be Chelsea. We talk by phone or in person regularly to compare relevant news items and decide which ones I'll investigate using my confidential sources and software tools. Then I give her my report that you and she can use however you think best."

Erika paused for him to try a typical ploy used by most journalists.

"What do you think might be relevant after that London Times editorial?"

"I'll be happy to tell Chelsea after you give me a contract."

"Fair enough. Chelsea will call you when you can pick it up. But how much will it cost?"

"The contract I emailed to Chelsea will tell you, and it'll be worth every pound and pence you pay."

"I like your style. I'll leave the details up to you two."

Chelsea spoke first after he left.

"My career is zooming, thanks to you. How can I repay you?"

"Just be a great London friend."

"Well, that gives me an idea. You must like sports and exercise a lot, because you look really fit. How would you like to be on my netball team? We play in a league set up by local fitness centers."

"What's netball?"

"It's an easier form of basketball that London females like. It's played on a basketball court, but the court is divided into three zones, and the seven players of each team have to stay in their assigned zones. Only players assigned to the zones under the basket can shoot, and there's no backboard. There's no dribbling; players can take only one-and-a-half steps before passing it. And it's not as rough as regular basketball. You'll catch on quick. You want to join?"

"Sure, and I can play whenever I have the time. Why don't you tell me when the next game will be when I pick up the contract?"

"That's perfect."

Erika stood before saying,

"I'll Email you my contract by the end of the day…"

Lily spoke first when walking back.

"Why don't we watch some netball videos that explain the rules while showing a game being played?"

"That's a great idea. And you can play if the situation arises. Everyone thinks you're a Londoner, so they'll assume you played in your younger years."

"Yes, indeed. That's the plan."

"OK, and I'll say what Chelsea's boss said to me—I like your style."

Clive didn't answer when she called after lunch, so she left a message saying she'd call tomorrow morning and then worked on the New York Times contract, which she Emailed late that afternoon. When a call came while suiting up to run, she guessed it would be Chelsea, but instead it was Clive.

"I was planning to call you tomorrow, but this call obviates it. My network contacts agreed with my editorial and are eager to see how I extend it."

"Mine do too. When could we meet to compare ideas for building on it?"

"I've blocked out Wednesday morning."

"Good. Why don't Lily and I meet with you at eight in your office? I'll even bring some biscuits."

"And I'll have a Karma Cola for both of you. See you then."

Erika decided to call Chelsea tomorrow and have Lily teach her netball that evening. After looking and listening for an hour, she said,

"I know enough to hold my own in the first game. And you can give me more pointers when we're playing."

"You won't need many. Your quick learning and exercising should make you a natural at netball."

"I hope so, but we'll see when Chelsea gets things going."

Chelsea did that on Tuesday afternoon when she called.

"My boss signed the contract. When do you want to pick it up?"

"How about Friday afternoon?"

"I'll be here, and if you're free Friday evening, how about playing your first netball game? Just bring a T-shirt and a pair of shorts."

"Where'll we play, and at what time?"

"At my fitness center, which is close to where I live in Abbey Wood. Our game starts at seven and lasts an hour."

"How'll we get there, and how long will it take?"

"I can get there to and from the News Building by either bus or Tube, and we'll take the Tube because it's quicker. It takes about twenty minutes. Trains come and go often, and we'll take the Tube and the interconnected Elizabeth Line."

"Is your neighborhood safe? What's it like?"

"We wouldn't be living there if it weren't. It's a lower-middle-class neighborhood with a mix of Victorian terrace houses and modern apartment buildings. Plenty of shopping and pubs too. The team usually goes to one close by afterward."

"You said 'we'. Who's included?"

"I live with my roommate, Daisy, who's also on the team."

Fighting the urge to ask more questions, Erika said,

"Sounds like a fun evening. I've been watching some netball videos, so I'm all set."

"Good, but let me tell you the rule change our league makes. Any player can score if they're in their zone, which makes games more exciting."

"I'll bring Lily too."

"That's fine. See you Friday afternoon."

As expected, Clive and the conference room were ready for Erika and Lily. After sipping and nibbling while chatting courteously for ten minutes, Clive shifted to the business at hand.

"All my network contacts see danger ahead because of what the U.S.-Russia Alliance might do. They say it has started an undeclared war against the EU, and we must bolster our military to push back against any aggression. We must also coordinate with China on how to do that."

Clive paused for Erika.

"My network says the same, labeling it 'the U.S.-Russia Alliance versus the World for economic and political domination.' It's afraid the Alliance will seek dominance by using its power to control key resources. Here's an example—rare earths and other minerals dug up in Antarctica."

"That's a novel way of analyzing the danger. What do you propose?"

"Let's develop a prompt I'll use to generate another report for you, and let's focus on energy, minerals, and biotech vaccines…"

Just before she and Lily left four hours later, she told Clive to expect his report no later than the end of next week.

"That will do just fine, but what will you do if the White House says something new?"

"Not to worry. I'll add it to the prompt…"

This time on the walk back, Erika spoke first.

"Electra-C will be pleased how all the pieces are fitting together. Guess what the next one will be?"

"You already have Indira, Clive, and Chelsea, so the next one must be Monet."

"You got it, and while running this afternoon, I'll plan what to say when I call her tomorrow. It'll be just enough so she'll understand why we'll meet at her Washington office. I'll call the A-Team on Saturday to arrange our travel back to the Deus Lab."

Lily asked,

"When do you plan to call Electra-C?"

"When do you think I should?"

"When we're back in London after meeting with Monet."

"I'm pleased with your answer. You're thinking more and more like me."

Lily smiled before saying,

"Whether you say 'like me' or 'like I,' the grammar is correct."

Erika laughed before replying.

"You're the best combination of office manager and personal assistant there is. Pretty soon, you'll be the only editor I need. How 'bout I show you my Monet script after I write it?"

"I'll be ready when you are…"

Although Erika had memorized the script, she kept it in front of her when she called Monet on Thursday at noon London time, which is seven in Washington. Monet didn't answer, so she left a message saying she'd call again at five and kept busy by working on Clive's prompt until she placed the call. This time, Monet answered.

"Hello, Erika. I recognized your number. How have you been?"

"Keeping busy, trying to keep up with the White House announcements. I imagine you have too."

"Yes, and everyone in my network finds them disturbing, but no one is willing to predict where they are leading. What do your contacts say?"

"To read the London Times editorial by Clive Milton that came out last week. By any chance, have you read it?"

"No. What does it say?"

"You need to read it, and that's why I'm calling. Thanks to my contacts, I see how the editorial builds on my press release, and I have ideas that will help the Indian African Alliance, but we need to meet at your office."

"Are you still staying at the Deus Lab?"

"Yes, and as soon as I know my schedule, may I call you between now and the end of the month to arrange a date?"

"That will be fine. Who should join us?"

"Only Alonzo until we decide how to proceed. Oops, I forgot to ask, how is he?"

"He helps me when I find something for him, but I think he would like to do more."

"Well, depending on our decision, his wish might come true. I'll call again soon. Bye-bye."

Erika turned to Lily when the call ended.

"Monet knows nothing about who you are, the business we've started, or where we're living, so we'll have to make up a believable story. How does this sound—I'm an independent political consultant, and when I met you on a London assignment, we decided to work together on a project-by-project basis?"

"That should work. It's close to the truth, which makes it easier on ourselves because we won't trip over any lies."

"Great answer. I couldn't have said it any better…"

Erika kept busy on Friday by switching among running prompts, watching netball videos, and thinking about what to say to Chelsea at her office. Erika reminded Lily before they left.

"We never want to give away too much information about our professional or personal lives. After she gives me the signed contract, I'll say we'll meet again soon so I can give her a customized report, and when we leave for the game, we'll stick only to small talk, OK?"

"I understand, and I'll stay in the background when we get to the game."

"Great answer. Now, let's go…"

Everything began unfolding according to Erika's plans. As she expected, Chelsea's teammates were young, fit, and trim professional females who enjoyed life. Including Erika and

Chelsea, there were only seven players this evening. When Erika showed during warmups that she could play the game, the team huddled up to assign positions.

Chelsea said,

"Since this is her first game, Erika should start at the center position because it's the easiest. Later on, we can move her to another if she's ready." All agreed.

Easing into the flow of the game, Erika felt ready for more by halftime. Lily, who was also wearing shorts and a T-shirt, thought the same.

"Tell Chelsea to put you in the goal attack position so you can try shooting." The team did that when the second half started.

When Erika scored a goal in the fourth quarter, her teammates told her to keep shooting because that might even the score, which she did with two minutes to go, but she twisted her ankle doing so and limped to the sidelines. When the team huddled, she said,

"Seven players are better than six; why don't you let Lily play the center position?"

Even though Lily looked more middle-aged than fit, they did so. The opposing players must have thought the same, because they ignored her. And that was their game-changing mistake.

With ten seconds remaining, both sides seemed ready to settle for a tie. When the opposing player holding the ball lobbed a lazy pass toward her center, Lily made a lightning-fast interception, took a giant leap toward the opponent's goal, and lofted a shot on an arc that nestled the ball into the net as time expired.

When teammates recovered from the shock of Lily's astounding score, they rushed to hug her. She smiled but let the others do the talking. Erika's words ended the celebration.

"We'd like to join you at the pub, but Lily needs all the rest she can get. She and I have a busy day planned for tomorrow. How 'bout we do that next time?"

Everyone agreed.

Chapter 10
January 2239

"A Cold War Heating Up"

Although Erika's ankle bothered her when she awoke the next morning, it didn't stop her from suiting up to run. Doing so with Lily standing next to her, she turned on a radio to check weather conditions, which had become threatening.

When ready to leave, she said,

"I should be back before the rain starts blowing but keep listening and tell me the latest news and weather. I wish I didn't have to run on a sore ankle, but I gotta stay in shape. That's why netball's easy for me. You don't have to worry about keeping fit, but we'll never tell Chelsea's team, even if they ask why you played so well. Do you wanna play again?"

"I should ask what you think, but I'll give the answer. No, I want to stay in the background."

Erika laughed, then said,

"Do you think I should skip the morning run?"

"Cognitively and physically, yes, but emotionally no. You'll feel guilty if you do; besides that, the endorphins make you feel good, so have at it…"

Running a lesser distance more than offset her slower speed, which brought her home just as the rains blew in. She thought Lily would look happy, but that wasn't the case. Before she could ask why, what Lily said gave the answer.

"The White House just announced that the United States and Russia are leaving the United Nations. I think you better change whatever you had planned for the day."

"Change the 'you' to 'us'; we'll start doing it after I shower and have some oatmeal."

They spent the morning first listening to additional media reports about the White House bomb shell and then calling the A-

Team to arrange for travel back to the Deus Lab. They would have plenty of time for packing because the A-Team would pick them up late Sunday afternoon, which meant they would arrive by midday Tuesday.

After lunch, Lily sat next to Erika while she ran Clive's updated prompt, speaking only when Erika asked for help. By the end of the afternoon, she had an interim prompt report.

Socio-Political Forecast for the London Times Prompt

- **By withdrawing both U.S and Russia from the UN, the U.S-Russia indicates it has started a new Cold War.**
- **Expect them to escalate it to actual military conflict if the other nations don't push back.**
- **European nations should leave the United Nations and form a new one headquartered in a European city.**
- **The EU and China should establish an informal EU-Chinese Alliance to counter the strength of their opponent.**
- **Expect Canada to sever economic ties to the U.S.**
- **Expect the EU-Chinese Alliance to lobby the rest of the world to boycott U.S. and Russian oil.**
- **Expect a nucleus of concerned United States congresspeople to form a new political party that will counter the U.S. government's turn toward authoritarianism.**
- **Expect the U.S.-Russian Alliance to flood the media with fake news, attempting to paralyze its enemies.**
- **Expect the new Indian African Alliance to partner with the EU and China in a manner that provides a defensive posture against the Aggressor.**

After showing it to Lily, who said nothing, Erika said,

"I'll tell Clive when I call him on Monday that his report will include the latest breaking news, but I won't give any details until I send it. I might call Chelsea too."

"What about Monet and Electra-C?"

"I'll call Monet from the Deus Lab, but I won't call Electra-C until we're back in London. I want us to do as much on our own before getting her involved. How do you like that?"

"I do, and I think Electra-C will too."

As Erika had hoped, the A-Team whisked them to the Deus Lab like she had planned, allowing her to call both Clive and Chelsea while en route and to adjust what she would say when meeting with Monet and Alonzo.

Although Lily had driven to Washington the last time, Jason-S did so this time so Erika and Lily could rehearse for the meeting. Erika also napped because they had left at two a.m. to arrive at Monet's office in the Zimbabwean embassy by nine.

Monet hid her surprised expression, but Alonzo couldn't, which showed when he asked, once the foursome was sitting at a conference room table.

"Who's with you?"

Looking satisfied after Erika recited her concocted story, he said,

"I'll get you a Coke, but I've heard Londoners like tea. Would Lily like that instead?"

Lily answered,

"Why, thank you, but I just finished some before we parked."

"OK, I'll be right back with Erika's Coke."

Erika popped the top when he returned. Monet began the conversation after she had taken a couple of sips.

"The latest White House revelation regarding abandoning the United Nations has heightened the worry of everyone in my network. After studying the London Times editorial, Alonzo and I now understand the gravity of the situation. I imagine your network does too. You mentioned you have some ideas for dealing with this U.S.-Russian Alliance threat. What do you propose?"

"My network has a list that covers more than even you can handle, so let's talk about the most important one for our Indian African Alliance and the United States. You need to recruit a nucleus of concerned congresswomen that will form a new political party that will counter the government's turn toward authoritarianism."

Not even Monet could hide the shock that now showed in her wordless gasp. When she recovered enough, she started asking questions Erika knew would be coming.

"Why congresswomen, and why a new party?"

"Plenty of political historians blame male egos for causing political upheavals. It's time for women to take control."

"Why a new party? We already have four?"

"Because they are controlled by a collective elite that works for the establishment embodied in the U.S.-Russian Alliance, not for the people. They crave raw power. Only a new party can unseat them. This new party will support democratic and traditional American values, DEI initiatives blended with Meritocracy, and a dedication to Isocracy, which is a form of government invented by ancient Greek philosophers where all citizens have equal political power. We're even proposing its name—Matriarchate Party.

This time, Alonzo asked the question.

"What does matriarchate mean?"

"Matriarchate is an adjective derived from the noun Matriarchy, which is a social system in which women hold all the positions of power and privilege. In a broader sense, it can also extend to moral authority, social privilege, and control of property."

Erika knew she had said enough because Monet's shocked expression had changed to one of understanding, as did the steely resolve in her voice.

"This can happen if I recruit the right congresswomen, but I'll need help. I assume you and Lily will assist me while mustering international support."

"That's the plan, and we can begin implementing it by holding a covert meeting with the congresswomen you trust, along with your trusted advocates for the Indian African Alliance."

Erika's words galvanized Alonzo to say,

"Monet's gonna need my security services because there's plenty of risk involved."

Erika nodded in Alonzo's direction before turning toward Monet.

"Precisely. How long will it take you to arrange a covert meeting?"

"At least a month. Why don't we take a ten-minute recess and then explore some other ideas until noon?"

"Good, and then Lily and I must leave, so why don't I call next week to compare progress?"

"That should work for all of us…"

Erika relaxed on the drive back to the Deus Lab while Lily sat next to Jason-S, letting him tell her about the nuances of driving on Interstate 95 as well as in DC and Manhattan. She didn't feel like going to bed when they arrived at nine, so with Lily sitting close, she arranged for their A-Team return to London after grabbing a snack and then invoked Electra-C's avatar, which waited for Erika to speak.

"I was going to contact you when Lily and I get back to London, which will be the day after tomorrow, but I'm too keyed up to wait because all my meetings went according to plan. Neither Clive nor Monet could add anything to what I already know. Can you think of anything I should add to the latest prompt you ran for me?"

"We have included all the relevant media news, which means you should discuss with Clive his customized socio-political report. Let him tell you what to add."

"If he has something useful, we'll run another report. If not, I won't, and either way, I'll give Chelsea only selected bullet points. I can't think of anything else, other than to let you know Lily's making life better and better for me."

"And I forecast that will continue. I believe she will agree. Contact me if not."

Electra-C disappeared before Erika could reply, so she turned to Lily and said,

"Whatcha think?"

"There's no need to contact Electra-C about me."

"I thought so, so now I can sleep worry-free. We'll pick up here tomorrow."

Lily gave a tiny smile when saying,

"Indeed, we will, and after that, so will the A-Team."

Erika's full-bodied smile came with her reply.

"I couldn't have said that better myself."

Erika picked up again in London on Thursday by Emailing Clive's report in the morning and calling late that afternoon. When he said he liked the report but wanted to discuss it, she said,

"How about in your office tomorrow at eight A.M.?"

"Perfect, and I'll supply all the snacks. See you then."

Clive had biscuits and beverages available on the conference room's credenza behind the table. He let Erika snack while he chatted casually for several minutes before beginning his interrogation.

"I must say, this Prompt Report is jolly thorough. Its forecast has more points than the sum of what my contacts and I could come up with. How do you manage it?"

"I've already told you my proprietary software comes up with them by analyzing Big Data, while my clients may think of others."

"May I ask who they are?"

"You may, but I won't tell. That's confidential."

"Very well, but will you tell me if you have something from them that is not in my Report?"

"Yes, and it extends point number six."

Clive paraphrased while reading.

"That's the one about a group of congresspeople forming a new political party."

Erika continued as soon as he stopped.

"My most trusted confidential sources in Washington tell me that a covert group of congresswomen will form the Matriarchate Party. It supports democratic and traditional American values, DEI initiatives blended with Meritocracy, and a dedication to Isocracy. You probably know the definition of Matriarchy but ask me if you don't remember."

Clive nodded before saying,

"How intriguing, putting all the power in the hands of women. Homer reported that Greek mythology talked about Amazon warrior women living northeast of Ancient Greece during the later Bronze Age, and the first European explorers in South America fought pitched battles with tribes of female warriors, whom he likened to the Amazons of Greek mythology. Hence the name Amazon River."

Not to be outdone, Erika chimed in.

"Ancient Egypt had two famous queens—Nefertiti and Cleopatra—as did Mesopotamia. And I should include all the queens of England. What about China?"

"It has had only one female ruler—Empress Wu Zeitan at the start of the 8th century. And in all these examples, men still held most of the power."

Erika regained control by saying,

"I'll tell you more later about what they're thinking after we walk through each bullet point..."

By the time they finished, Clive said,

"You wore me out. I need to share the Report with my network. Perhaps that will stimulate new items to put in a prompt."

"Call me when you have them. In the meantime, I'll also look for some."

Lily spoke first on the walk back.

"You look so pleased. Clive's comment about your wearing him out is an oblique compliment. You should go for a run if your ankle has recovered before picking items for Chelsea."

"That's what I'll do before Emailing them and planning to call her next week to ask if she has anything to add. And after I send the EMail, we can cruise until next Monday. Maybe you can think about some weekend sightseeing."

"Will do..."

Increasing the distance each day, Erika ran the pre-sprain distance on Saturday and was ready to tell Lily the good news, but when she bounded into the office, Lily's concerned look made her ask,

"What's wrong?"

"We won't want to do any sightseeing this weekend. The radio reported the latest White House disruption—the President just pitched the entire Supreme Court into jail."

Erika leaned toward as her mouth jerked open, but no words came out until she pulled back, shook her head sideways, and said,

"Holy Jeezus. This'll change all our plans. We better get ready because the Cold War is starting to heat up...."

Chapter 11
March 2239

"A Matter of Taste"

Erika thought nonstop about the ramifications of the U.S.-Russian Alliance's threats. Everyone in her network said the international political landscape would change, but no one knew how. Desperate for ideas after three weeks, she invoked Electra-C's avatar and pleaded her case.

"No one, not even Clive or Monet, will make even a guess. They say it's my job, and they're right. I've tried my best to think of things I can add to the prompt when running the socio-political forecast app, but nothing gives me anything other than what came up on the socio-political report I gave Clive two months ago."

Erika paused until her trembling lips, heaving chest, and emerging tears subsided.

"I'm not as smart as I thought I was getting, and I must be a big disappointment to you, so please, give me some suggestions that'll get me going again in the right direction."

Electra-C spoke in a tone matching her empathetic expression.

"You never disappoint me when you try your best, and I know you are during these extraordinary times. Here are suggestions for proceeding. Expect the Alliance to use military force against all opponents and the European Union to boycott American and Russian oil. Draw some conclusions by watching the protest demonstrations in the U.S. and reporter interviews. Do the same in London. Contact me again if you need additional help after that. Now, cheer up and proceed, using your considerable talent and resources."

With Lily at her side, Erika started watching numerous media telecasts of the FBI and CIA dispersing protestors. The president mobilized the National Guard when the crowds became too large because the local police refused.

Seeing this for the first time, Erika folded her shoulders while gaping at the monitor and said,

"It's appalling how they're busting protestors' heads and reporters' cameras."

Lily said,

"Do you think it'll shrink the number of protestors?"

"Maybe not. The number at each protest might decrease, but the number of American cities holding them might increase. We'll have to wait and see."

Having collected enough new prompt ideas to generate a set of socio-political reports that she would share with Clive and Chelsea, Erika decided to go for a run before calling them. While watching her suit up, Lily said,

"The weather's nice, so why don't you try running through Hyde Park this afternoon? It has jogging trails that will take you past some of the tourist attractions I've already told you about, and you'll run through Knightsbridge on the way."

"That's a great idea. I can combine sightseeing with working out. See you later…"

Every step took her thoughts closer to the moment and farther from work.

Warm sunlight makes running even more stress-relieving… today feels like late spring… maybe climate change is bringing spring earlier to London…

As she crossed the Thames, she focused on the neighborhood.

Wow, Knightsbridge sure is an upscale neighborhood… those grand Victorian homes with leafy gardens say so… I just passed a swanky shopping mall… I bet Harrods department store and the nearby restaurants bring in lots of tourists, as does the Victoria and Albert Museum… good that street sign points the way…

The jogging trails were even better than she expected.

It feels like I'm running on a cushioned trail winding through manicured fields with trimmed bushes and trees… no wonder I see lots of wildlife… look, two geese with a gaggle of goslings right behind… they're the fowl metaphor for London families out for a stroll.

Erika's thoughts shifted abruptly.

Humans are the only species that must deliberately exercise to keep in shape. Nature's survival of the fittest takes care of that for all others... I bet it does the same for those that are dumber or have mental problems... society frowns on those words today... people don't have mental problems... they have challenges... I'll have to ask Electra-C what neuroscientists say about tinkering with our gene pool.

Her thoughts shifted again when she passed another signpost.

One path'll take me to Marble Arch, another to Speakers' Corner, another to the Rose Garden, and another to the Serpentine... I'm passing by iconic British landmarks...

By the time Erika returned home, she felt fully relaxed and ready to call Clive soon after she showered and had a light supper.

After he gave his usual courteous greeting, she said,

"I'm ready to email your updated report. Shall I explain it to you in person?"

"Before I answer, please tell me what new insights it provides."

"OK, here are the biggies. The White House will order more troops to quell riots spreading to more cities and will start arresting reporters. European governments will ban U.S. oil and Russian gas along with consumer goods, impacting the cost of living, and major European cities will hold protests similar to those in America. Finally, the EU will form a new United Nations located in Bern, the capital of Switzerland."

"Please send me the report, and I'll ask my network for their comments. Why don't we meet after I do that?"

"Good idea. Please call me when you're ready..."

Erika maintained momentum by calling Chelsea, speaking as soon as she answered.

"Hi Chelsea, it's Erika. I've got some new socio-political points for you and your boss. Why don't we meet at your office on Friday?"

"That's the day after tomorrow. I'll ask my boss if that's OK and call you if it isn't. And either way, would you like to go to a fine arts lecture that evening?"

"Where will it be?"

"In Knightsbridge at six-thirty in the home of the lecturer. She writes for the London Fine Arts Society's journal and even has a blogging site. Why don't you search for it and tell me what to expect?"

"OK, and will we take the Tube to get there?"

"That'll be the fastest way."

"How do you know?"

"My roommate, Daisy, is a member of the Young Women's Chapter of the Fine Arts Society, which sometimes holds meetings there. She's never attended anything there but gave me directions. When she told me she's not going because she doesn't feel good, I immediately thought about inviting you and Lily. I think the topic is something about music."

"This should be fun. I'll see you at four Friday afternoon…"

Erika kept all activities perking through Thursday and Friday morning, but Lily interrupted her train of thought when she received an unexpected call. After saying,

"This is Erika Kincaid; how may I help?" a deep British man's voice said,

"Clive Milton called me yesterday for my thoughts on some new insights regarding what the U.S.-Russian Alliance might do. He wouldn't give me all the details, but instead said I could subscribe to your consulting service."

Erika picked up when he paused.

"What would you like?"

"A multi-client contract. Two other reporters on Milton's network would like to meet with you. Would you be willing to meet with the three of us like you're doing with Milton?"

"The three of you must sign a contract."

"How much will your service cost?"

"I will put it in the contract."

"How will it compare with Milton's?"

"Each client's information is confidential."

Erika paused, knowing that the first person to talk would lose the negotiation.

Fifteen seconds elapsed before the fellow said,

"When would you like to meet the three of us in my office?"

"Monday works for me, if it works for you. Please give me the three names, your address, and phone number."

"Very well. Here's all the information…"

When she rushed to tell the news after the call ended, Lily said,

"Please remember that our clients will expect exclusive services to cost more. In our case, they'll never know how we'll combine all their ideas to increase the breadth and depth of the reports."

Erika's flushed cheeks and glowing eyes came with her words.

"Both of us know the tricks of combining negotiations and marketing, and I'll make sure we under-promise and over-perform. I hope the lady speaking tonight does the same. And that reminds me—I better check her blogging site."

Erika spent enough time before leaving to form an opinion she kept to herself.

She sure seems pleased with her BA in Fine Arts from the London University of the Arts. She also has an MS in Musicology
from the London College of Music, so she must be smart. Music's not my strong suit, so I'll just do the listening. I'll have something to eat too, because she'll be serving a catered buffet. I'm sure it'll be tasty…

Erika hid her delight that Chelsea's boss didn't join the meeting. After handing her a redacted version of Clive's report, she recommended that her boss let her interview typical Londoners to compare reactions to those of Americans.

Before the threesome left at five, Erika told them about the evening.

"The presentation's title sounds high-brow to the max—Redefining Classical Music: A Synthesis of Linguistic and Auditory Sensations Fitting all Periods. We can mingle when we get there to find out what others know. Good thing we'll have dinner between hearing the music and listening to the lecture."

Erika and Lily followed Chelsea from the office to the Tube and then to the presenter's home. Chelsea gasped before clanging the brass knocker on its massive wooden door.

"This looks like more than a home; it's like the estate of a baroness. We'd better watch our step."

A properly attired butler led them to a reception area, where people could pick up a program notes pamphlet. Erika estimated a crowd of sixty and counted only five fellows, all well past middle age. She saw only five women who could be younger than forty, and even they were dressed for a party.

She could feel her ears turning red and sweat forming on the back of her neck when Chelsea whispered,

"Maybe we should leave."

Erika was about to agree, but then she remembered something Electra-C had told her long ago.

"No way. No one knows who we are, so follow my lead and just pretend you belong."

As soon as she began chatting with a nearby couple, Erika felt her embarrassment and nervousness melt away. Chelsea did the same while Lily stayed with Erika.

When the lights flickered, the butler ushered the crowd into an enormous living room containing five rows with enough seating capacity for the crowd. Behind the podium stood an elegant-looking woman who began speaking once the crowd-buzzing white noise stopped.

"Good evening, and welcome to my program. I'll begin by playing a mix of medieval, baroque, renaissance, enlightenment, modern, and post-modern music listed in your pamphlet, which should take forty-five minutes. Afterward, please follow the butler to the buffet table, fill your plates, and return for my lecture. Your pamphlet also lists what is being served. And now, let the music play."

The longer it played, the more fervent Erika's silent prayer became.

Jeezus, I hope the music stops soon… I don't recognize any of it… and it's getting harder to listen to…

When Chelsea whispered much the same, Erika gave her the shush sign with one hand while gently squeezing her arm with the other.

Mercifully, the music stopped, and when the audience started forming a buffet line, Erika kept drifting toward the end, hoping that her appetite might build, but it didn't, so she put a dab of each entree on her plate before returning to Chelsea and Lily. Then she asked for a description of what she was about to taste, which Chelsea regurgitated from the pamphlet.

"Let's see, I recognize haggis because it's packed into the lining of a sheep's stomach. It's the national dish of Scotland and contains ground-up sheep's liver, heart, and lungs combined with spices, minced beef, onions, and mutton suet.

"There's also gelled eel. Too bad the pieces are so large. I could actually see the eyes of its head staring at me. There's also an enormous sliced beef tongue served with horseradish.

"And I recognize head cheese because it's served in a hollowed-out pig's head. It's made from animal brains and is—" Erika's gagging stopped whatever Chelsea was about to say. The combination of entree descriptions and flavors overpowered her digestive system.

She grabbed her stomach, doubled over, and dry heaved for twenty seconds. Shocked by the sight and sound, people sitting nearby started yelling for help, and the butler came running.

"Dear me, I shall summon the doctor."

Erika had recovered enough to stammer,

"Th-thanks, but no. Uh-I feel good enough to go now."

"What was the matter?"

Staggering to her feet, she said,

"I-uh I don't know for sure, but something I tasted or heard didn't agree with my stomach. I'm sorry I caused such a commotion."

Her companions rose, and Lily steadied her while the butler escorted them out.

Though she didn't recover her appetite, Erika's sense of humor had returned by the time the trio waited for their train on the Tube's platform. She said,

"Chelsea was right. We should have left earlier, and I should have followed her warning to watch my step. I should have gone anywhere but the buffet. Let's keep this episode to ourselves."

Chelsea smiled before replying.

"I didn't like how the food tasted, either. I guess you could say I had more than a stiff upper lip."

The sound of a train coming stopped her from saying more, but as it coasted to a stop, Lily added the last word.

"How lucky I sampled nothing but the music. Now I know what to avoid, and Erika looks like she'll be back to normal by tomorrow."

"I hope so. We have lots to do...."

Chapter 12
June 2239

"On the Move Again"

Erika and Lily had plenty to do as soon as their clients saw the damage being done across the globe by the U.S.-Russian Alliance. Clive found more items for Erika to put in his prompt-generated reports, as did Chelsea and her boss. She also took part in Chelsea's interviews and helped new clients interpret their customized reports.

Monet contacted Erika in early June, asking her to meet with the congresswomen she had recruited, so they returned to the Deus Lab. Soon after arriving, Erika called a meeting with the androids in charge.

As Erika and Lily sat on one side of the conference table with Indy-M, Indy-S, and Jason-S on the other, she mused while sipping a Coke and felt a relaxing warmth spread through her.

Of course, I'm the only one snacking. I often forget my androids don't need to, can work twenty-four-seven, and can handle whatever comes up. Let's find out what's happening here.

Erika put the can on the table and straightened her shoulders before starting the meeting.

"You always have the Lab in tip-top shape. What's the status of the projects you're coordinating?"

Indy-M spoke first.

"My projects include all your business ventures on American Indian reservations."

"Has the U.S.-Russian Alliance affected them?"

"Only two—vaccine manufacturing and development, and genetic R&D. Indy-S will explain further."

"I coordinate vaccine activities, which the White House embargo on all vaccine exports has curtailed. Jason-S will explain the genetic research piece. The White House just empowered the FDA to control all domestic genetic R&D. They can't control what the Deus Lab does because Indian reservations are currently outside its jurisdiction, but that can change whenever the U.S.-Russian Alliance wants."

Erika's frown and quickening pulse preceded her words.

"Hmm, is there a workaround?"

Jason-S answered.

"Deus Lab vaccine manufacturing and development, and genetic R&D should be shut down and moved to a new offshore Deus Lab."

Erika grimaced while tugging her right earlobe.

"Let me get all this straight. We keep this Deus Lab location open so Indy-M can continue running my domestic operations, but we'll open another somewhere else for vaccine stuff and genetic R&D. Who'll run it?"

"Indy-S and I have the skills to coordinate moving and running it."

Erika felt her skin tingle as she leaned toward him.

"You're right, and I know the next step. Meeting adjourned."

With Lily standing behind, Erika invoked Electra-C's avatar after hurrying to a workstation. Once it appeared, she rocked back and forth while sitting as her wavering words spilled out.

"I hope you overheard my last conversation, because I need your help. What's the best way to relocate the Deus Lab?"

"Hire the A-Team and put Jason and Indy-S in charge. And I'll answer your next question, so you don't need to ask where to locate it. I shall lease a facility in a European city and assist when needed."

Erika exhaled while bowing toward the monitor and saying,

"Thank you, thank you. That'll let me concentrate on my Monet meeting."

"That is my intention. Start now and contact me afterward."

Lily spoke after Erica-C vanished.

"Would you like to start now or after you run?"

Erika's happy look showed she knew what Lily would like.

"Afterward. I always think better after I get a jolt of endorphins. See ya later..."

Running alternately in the warm sunlight or cool shade of the trees lining reservation trails she knew well, Erika did all the concentration necessary. When she returned, Lily and Jason-S sat across from her at the snack table and did nothing but listen.

"I already know what to say and do at Monet's meeting. And like we've done before, Jason-S drives while Lily sits next to him, and I snooze in the back seat. I'll call Monet so she can tell me the day and time. And that'll do it until we return..."

Erika and Lily entered Monet's Zimbabwean embassy office fifteen minutes before the meeting so Monet could give them background information. She did the minimal amount of chit-chat before launching into what Erika needed.

"According my sample of congresspeople, The U.S.-Russian Alliance disruptions have split Capitol Hill into two camps, divided eighty percent for and twenty percent against, but according to my best contact in the foreign diplomat corps—and I'm quoting him—embassies are ninety-nine and forty-four one-hundredths percent against, which I imagine would be the same for the White House Press Corps and beyond. And according to congresswomen who were willing to state their opinions, an overwhelming majority in all but the now-in-power Guardian Party oppose it."

When Monet paused to gauge Erika's reaction, her words matched tightened fists and a curt nod.

"That jibes with my intuition, which also tells me anyone who opposes the Alliance is about to enter the danger zone. No wonder you had trouble recruiting congresswomen willing to champion our cause. What progress have you made?"

"Enough to call this meeting. I have eight, one senator and one representative from each party. And the President trusts the two coming from the Guardian Party, so they'll know what disruptions the two most problematic Departments—Homeland Security and Government Efficiency—are about to cause. It's time we go to the conference room."

Monet led the way.

Monet sat at the head of the table, with Erika on her left and Lily on her right. As Erika had expected, the eight congresswomen trickled in one by one and sat silently in one of the eight other chairs around the table. Monet began the meeting when all the chairs were occupied.

"This is the first official, though covert, meeting of the brave congresswomen willing to champion the formation of a new political party—the Matriarchate Party. When I met privately with each, I explained why it is needed and what its guiding principles will be, but for reasons of everyone's safety, I never mentioned names.

"And before I ask you to introduce yourself, let me do that for the consultants sitting alongside me. To my right is Erika Kincaid, and to my left is her partner, Lily Lloyd. And now, proceeding clockwise on my left, please tell us who you are."

Erika jotted down the name, party affiliation, and her impression for each. When number eight had spoken, Monet said,

"Now, I want each person to tell what disturbing actions the White House might make within the next two months, and we'll go in this party order—Democratic, Regen, Republican, and finally Guardian. There is no need for you to take notes, because Erika will record them."

Erika multitasked by talking to herself while typing what she heard into her laptop.

They're repeating many points, but that makes my note-taking more thorough and accurate... and Monet's right. The Guardian Party congresswomen have more possible disruptions than the rest combined...

An hour had elapsed when Monet said,

"What a horrendous list of threats. Let's take a fifteen-minute break for coffee and whatever else you need to do. When we resume, Erika will summarize the most disruptive threats, and then I will lead our discussion to explore workarounds."

During the break, Erika uploaded to the interactive digital whiteboard what she considered the most pressing potential threats. She and Lily gazed at it, but said nothing, because Monet and the congresswomen had just returned.

Potential U.S.-Russian Alliance Disruptions

- Withholding Unemployment and Social Security Benefits from White House Opponents.
- Eliminating Courses and Departments at Universities that the White House doesn't like.
- Networking all Government, Corporate, and Private Citizens' Surveillance Cameras to spy everywhere.
- Creating the Department of Surveillance Agency.
- Seizing the Assets located in the U.S. of Foreign Governments and Corporations.
- Using military SWAT teams to capture political leaders while in their home countries.

Monet let the group stare at the whiteboard for twenty seconds before saying,

"I want to level set the word we'll be addressing for the rest of the morning, which is workaround. It is a bypass of a recognized problem or limitation in a system or policy. A workaround is typically a temporary fix that implies that a genuine solution to the problem is needed. But workarounds are frequently as creative as true solutions, involving outside-the-box thinking in their creation. And like we did before the break, Erika will record our ideas."

This time, Erika recorded what was spoken for the next three hours and would use a voice-to-writing translator for easier analysis when she returned home.

Monica ended the meeting at noon.

"I will review with each of you privately Erika's report, which, for reasons of safety, will not be distributed, but Erika will issue a press release meant to disguise the sensitive details like she did on another project so this time the media can broadcast to the world why we need a new political party I plan to—" a congresswoman waving her arms interrupted.

"That must have been the one about the Indian African Alliance. Now I see her connection to us. Sorry, what were you going to say?"

"That we will meet again covertly soon after the media tells the world it needs our Matriarchate Party…"

Erika waited for the congresswomen to leave before she would do the same after a final word with Monet, who was waiting in her office. When she entered, Monet's pacing and furrowed brow telegraphed her worried feelings, which she usually kept hidden.

"If the U.S.-Russian Alliance keeps pushing like it has, it'll push the world community even faster and further into the danger zone. I heard nothing encouraging during the workaround discussion. I hope you can find at least a smidge to build on."

"I'll start working on it and put how I extend them into the newsletter."

"Good. Send it for my approval ASAP. Then I can show it to my diplomatic and Indian-Africa Alliance network contacts. I might ask you to come back sooner."

Erika said,

"I'll keep you posted on progress," before hustling away.

Lily sat next to Jason-S on the drive back to the Deus Lab, but this time, Erika couldn't unwind in the back seat. Instead, she started running the translator to process what she had recorded, resting only long enough to re-energize.

Though darkness had fallen by the time they were back, Erika decided to run, hoping the exercise would remove the stress and stiffness from sitting and thinking too long and bring back happy feelings, but even after a shower and a can of Coke, she felt depressed. When she saw Erika just sitting and staring into space, Lily said,

"You should talk to Electra-C."

That roused Erika enough to say,

"Let's go to a workstation and do it."

When the avatar appeared, Lily spoke first.

"Erika doesn't look happy. Please give her some advice so she'll feel good again."

Electra-C nodded, then showed the hint of a smile before her calm words came.

"Let's have her summarize the day and how she feels now."

Erika roused herself enough to speak phlegmatically.

"It started OK. I knew what to do and say during the meeting, but by the end, not even Monet could offer anything substantial, and I had to produce something useful fast and on my own. I've started, but the pressure's depressing me and stopping my progress. If I could feel happy again, I'd move on."

When the length of Erika's pause signaled that she had said everything she wanted to, Electra-C's soothing tone added to the impact of her words.

"You are never alone. Through hard work, you've honed your natural talent into a clever and resourceful analyst who knows how to use resources and network with others to complete whatever's assigned. And you have me when you need something more."

Electra-C's pause encouraged Erika to ask,

"What do I need?"

"I will refresh your memory. You say you want to feel happy again, and philosophers say it is better to feel good. Happiness is ephemeral. Think back to the times you've enjoyed a chocolate milkshake. How did you feel?"

"Happy until I sucked out the last drop; then I felt sad."

"And how do you feel when helping Chelsea?"

"Like I'm glowing, radiating goodness."

Erika paused, but when Electra-C said,

"Please continue," the sparkle in her eyes and voice started to return.

"Now I see where this is going. Philosophers say we should live a good life, which sometimes might not be so happy, but it always leads to better things. If I remember what you taught me, Socrates says we live the good life by seeking truth, Plato says we live it by balancing our inner nature with reality, and Aristotle says we live it by developing our virtue-rich character. How's that?"

"Like you're ready to move on. Please summon me whenever you need another reminder. You know what to do to start moving on, so do it now."

Erika turned to Lily when the avatar vanished.

"Can you guess what we'll do?"

Lily chirped pertly,

"Why yes. We'll contact the A-Team for a ride back to London. How's that?"

"Perfect, and by the time we get there, we'll be ready to take the next steps by ourselves. All you need to do is follow me."

"And I know how to do that."

Chapter 13
July 2239

"On the Road Once More"

Electra-C's pep talk had erased Erika's depression, putting her back in action and doing everything Monet expected. Her newsletter caused activists to riot at social security and unemployment offices across America, roving bands of youths to blow up government surveillance systems, and civic-minded citizens to rip out home security cameras.

Chelsea's New York Times report not only scooped the news but also emboldened the major media companies to expose Washington's intentions, and Clive's editorial heightened Europe's concern about the U.S.-Russian Alliance.

However, the White House countered by spewing out false information that kept its opponents off balance and installing a "guilty until proven innocent" mandate for cases the President deemed critical for national security. He could also place the defendants in his showcase penitentiary, Alcatraz, and deny them access to a lawyer.

Erika knew the Administration would make these and additional moves, so she alerted Monet first before telling Clive and Chelsea. She also saw that none of the workarounds worked, which forced her to contact Electra-C.

When she described the situation, Electra-C said,

"Civil disobedience and peaceful demonstrations lack the muscle to stop the U.S.-Russian Alliance. The time has come to use force."

"But if we start firing weapons, the other side will fire more and bigger ones, and the EU doesn't have its military ready to pitch in."

"But consider cyberspace, not 3-D space. You have the Terminator Weapon and Cyber Torpedoes. It is time to deploy them. Do you remember how?"

"I think so—I pick the targets and you launch them. What do you think I should pick?"

"That is for you to decide. Contact me when ready."

"I will after I see what's happening elsewhere. And the first elsewhere is our new Deus Lab. Did you pick the location?"

"Switzerland, because it leads Western Europe's DNA research and development in biotechnology and genomics. Bern might have been the best city, but I selected the most suitable one close by."

"Why didn't you choose Bern? No, don't tell me, I know. It'll be the location of the new United Nations."

"Excellent. I chose Lausanne. Here's the address and the phone number. Now, please proceed."

Erika did that while peering at a map of Western Europe and pointing out city locations to Lily.

"Here's London, and here's Bern, southeast of London. If we drive, we'll go through Switzerland on the way. Let's check the distance and directions for doing so."

After searching the Web, she continued.

"It'll be about a six-hundred-mile drive, and we can sightsee along the way, and we get from England to France by loading the car on a shuttle train that crosses the English Channel by taking the twenty-three-mile Channel Tunnel underneath."

Lily pointed out,

"It would be faster and easier to fly. Why do you want to drive?"

A shallow sigh came before the answer.

"I did some driving in France and Germany with Terri, my dearly departed previous partner. We had a great time getting interviews done while sightseeing."

"Do you know that the UK and Ireland are the only Western European countries to drive on the left-hand side of the road? The car we'll rent in London will have a steering wheel on the right."

"That's good. We get to practice what it's like driving around old London town…"

The duo split driving duties on the way to Lausanne. Erika couldn't survey the scenery when behind the wheel, because she had to concentrate on the road and traffic, but she did when Lily was driving.

The gently rolling countryside's greenery looks so lush, no doubt helped by the combination of pleasant spring temperatures and rains. And the picturesque towns and villages look so culturally rich... We'll do our Switzerland sightseeing after touring the Deus Lab.

Erika commented to herself as she and Lily walked to the Deus Lab's entrance.

This R&D park is perfect. All the same-sized buildings are clean and modern. We won't be noticed.

Opening the door when Erika pushed the buzzer, Jason-S said,

"Please follow me to the conference room. Indy-S is already there. I will point you to the restroom if you need it."

After making a quick stop for Erika, they trooped into the conference room and took positions around the table.

Indy-S spoke immediately.

"Electra-C told us you would visit today. Before we discuss our activities, why don't we take you on a tour of the workstations?"

Erika asked,

"How many are there? What's their function? And what's their current status?"

Jason-S said,

"Five. I am responsible for two—the DNA Extraction Station, and the CRISPR Gene Snipping and Insertion Station. Indy-S handles the other three—the Cloning Station, Birth Station, and Growth Station. Please hold additional questions until after the tour, which will proceed in the order I mentioned."

Jason and Indy-S walked side by side, with Eika and Lily tandem right behind. Only Erika's inner voice spoke.

The DNA extraction station needs a sample of cheek cells, blood, hair, saliva, bone, or even mummified remains... then the CRISPR station snips gene segments out and can insert new ones... next, the cloning station inserts the new DNA into the nucleus of a generic egg cell, which then grows via the birth chamber into a newborn... and the growth station accelerates or decelerates growth to the physiological age desired via a suspension pod like the one NASA uses for space travel, but Indira's singular software controls it... I'm sure glad the tour's ending...

Erika grabbed a candy bar and Coke from a vending machine and snacked while Indy and Jason-S explained more about each station. When they finished, Indy-S said,

"Now you know the basics. Do you have more questions?"

Erika felt her face radiate heat before taking a deep breath and then saying,

"The stations are all set, but none have been used yet. Why not?"

"We are waiting for tissue samples, which start the entire process."

"OK, and how do you obtain them?"

"Ask Electra-C."

"OK, and what's the goal?"

"Ask Electra-C?"

"OK, and how do I fit in?"

"That is another question for Electra-C."

Erika fought the urge to use a sarcastic tone by tapping the knuckles of her right hand on the table for a moment before saying,

"Well, maybe you can answer this question—what Swiss sightseeing stops should we make on the drive back?"

"Surf the Web to find the answer."

"Well, I'll do that this minute. Then we're on our way..."

The duo detoured through Bern to start the journey home. Erika did the driving and spoke first.

"No wonder the UNESCO tour recommendation says Bern's the place to go. It labels the place a World Heritage Site... lots of tourists strolling along its medieval streets entered through picturesque arches and lined with sandstone buildings... we'll just drive by."

Lily did the rest of the talking.

"The city's historic charm shines through in the colorful fountains and beautifully preserved architecture... the sign says we're driving past the Zytglogge, which is Bern's iconic medieval clock tower. According to the UNESCO article, its astronomical clock and hourly mechanical puppet show attract lots of tourists… and there's another signpost pointing the way to Bear Park or the Rose Garden…"

Erika exited Bern two hours later, and when she reached the highway that would take them back to London, she let Lily drive all the way home.

Erika planned to call Electra-C the next morning, but a call from Chelsea came in before she could.

"Today's Saturday, and all of us have earned a break. Daisy and I are going to a dance club tonight. Do you and Lily wanna come?"

"Lily and I haven't done much dancing lately. Will we look silly on the dance floor?"

"Not at all. I haven't either. Daisy's the dancer. She picked one of the smaller Soho clubs that won't overwhelm us."

"Well, in that case, it's a great idea. What should we wear, and where and when should we meet?"

"Anything you can dance in. Here's the club's name and address. Let's meet out front at seven…"

Soon after the foursome sat at the table, Daisy led them to near the dance floor, and a waitress took their drink orders before Daisy started explaining club rules. They seemed obvious to Erika, so she listened while talking to herself.

Daisy picked the right time and place. The youngish crowd's still filtering in, and the DJ's just beginning to load the tunes into the mixer. Once upon a time, I did that for Cassie and Terri…

Dancing started when the music started, about forty-five minutes later. Daisy and Chelsea paired up with two fellows who came to the table, allowing Erika and Lily to watch the dancers' moves, which pulsing lights and video images playing on the wall behind the DJ made even more exciting.

The music was too loud for Erika to say anything to Lily, so she talked to herself.

I'm seeing moves that're different from what we saw on the Web this morning… I'll try to add them to the ones we practiced this afternoon…

Erika joined the crowd when a fellow tapped her on the shoulder and pointed toward the dancers. She hugged Lily before melting in with the other dancers.

The uncertainty in her head and the tenseness in the pit of her stomach began dissipating midway through the first tune and disappeared completely when she started mirroring her partner's moves in the third. When Chelsea and her partner danced alongside, they changed partners. Soon Daisy joined them, and the three couples continued.

Erika had lost track of the time when the music and strobe lights stopped, replaced by the ceiling lights and DJ's reverberating voice.

"Hurrah to all you movers and shakers. It's time for our Saturday night special contest, so clear the floor and get ready for my partner's instructions."

Several minutes later, an exotic, dark-skinned, and short-skirted female's sexy voice continued.

"I've been dancing and mingling on the floor and among the tables, noticing which of you might need a little encouragement, so I'm going to select three guys and three gals to join the DJ, who'll say more."

Erika pulled Lily close and yelped,

"I know she's gonna pick you. Do your best to win."

All eyes at the table followed the selector, who made Lily pick number six. When Lily stood to follow her, Chelsea yelled,

"Go get-em," Lily smiled.

The DJ said more when he had all six lined up next to him in the order picked.

"Each will dance solo for five minutes to the same medley that builds in tempo from start to end. Faster tempo means you can cut loose using your best moves. You'll dance in the order you're lined up. The audience will hold their applause until everyone's danced, and then I'll point to each of you. The audience's applause will pick the winner. And tonight's prize. The club pays the bar tab for the winner and everyone at the table. Are there questions? If not, let's begin."

Erika noticed the picking order appeared random. There was no pattern based on age or ability, but she guessed Lily was last because she was the oldest and pudgiest among the six. She also knew what would happen, but kept it to herself.

Lily started cautiously, using the simpler steps she had seen this afternoon or evening, but used increasingly intricate ones the longer the medley played. Her arm and leg positions synced with the sexy body positions, and she ended with a backspin lying on the floor before leaping to her feet and doing a back flip, landing on the floor with one leg extended forward and the other backward.

When she daintily rose to get back in line, the stunned silence was palpable, but the DJ kept things moving.

"Congratulations to all our fine contestants. I'm sure your applause will encourage them to keep dancing, so please give it up to each when I point."

Every contestant but Lily received polite applause. Lily's brought the club down. The selector took her and a waitress back to the table, where Lily received a collective hug. After the foursome sat, Erika glanced at her cell phone before saying,

"It's almost midnight, and I'm too pumped to do any more dancing. I say we call it a night."

Everyone agreed, and soon Chelsea and Daisy went their separate way.

Erika did the talking while she and Lily took the Tube home. And when they settled in, Erika ended the evening.

"I'll call Electra-C first thing in the morning. Then we'll find out her and Indira's intentions for us and the new Deus Lab," but Lily had the last word.

"Perhaps...."

Chapter 14
July 2239

"An Assignment from Indira"

Erika decided to call Electra-C first and exercise afterward, because she could think about what Electra-C said while on the run. With Lily sitting nearby and after invoking the avatar before summarizing what she had seen and heard while touring the Lausanne Deus Lab, Erika said,

"Indy and Jason-S know what to do with tissue samples and will start when they begin arriving, but they couldn't tell me their purpose or my role, so what's the deal?"

"The samples begin arriving when you start sending them, which is your initial role."

Erika squinted at the monitor while pursing her lips and stuttering,

"Wh-what? Hu-how am I supposed to do that?"

"You know the kinds of tissues to collect. I recommend hair or saliva before resorting to more intrusive techniques."

"Bu-but from whom or where?'

"Start with whom. Find four extraordinary people, two male and two female. When you have their samples, take them to the Deus Lab, and I'll answer your next question before you ask—extraordinary means they are talented physically, cognitively, or emotionally."

"Aha, now I get it. Those are the three personas you and I sometimes talk about. You told me that Indira plans to use the adaptive, three-person model of the brain when editing DNA to create a sub-species of hermaphroditic-parthenogenic females, but first, she has to eliminate the DNA editing problems that caused Cassandra's death. It sounds like she's done that."

"Correct. I will explain your additional roles after you have perfected the collection procedure."

"You've just given me another task I need to complete besides picking Cyber Torpedo targets. Which should I finish first?"

"Always finish the one that takes less time, so pick your targets."

Erika felt a sudden lightness in her chest. She gave a crisp nod and said,

"Will do, and I'll—" Electra-C disappeared before Erika could say more, but at least she saw her twinkly smile emerge before she did.

After running and showering, Erika sat with Lily, having a breakfast of oatmeal sprinkled with brown sugar and raisins that Lily had waiting, and did most of the talking between heaping spoonfuls.

"I've got some ideas I'll explain later for how to collect samples, but let's talk about your personas now. You demonstrated your superior physical persona last night at the dance club, and I think your cognitive persona's better than mine and what most people have, so let's see if you can draw something I can't—

a diagram of the Triune Brain Model."

"Why yes. Please give me a minute or two."

Lily began sketching after returning with a pen and pad of paper. When she finished ten minutes later, she showed it to Erika and waited for her to speak.

Triune Brain Model

- **Reptilian Brain Region is Physical Persona for Controlling Body Movement**
- **Limbic System Region is the Emotional Persona for Regulating Emotions and Feelings**
- **Neocortex Region is Cognitive Persona for Regulating Verbal, Logical, and Mathematical Activities**

PHYSICAL BRAIN

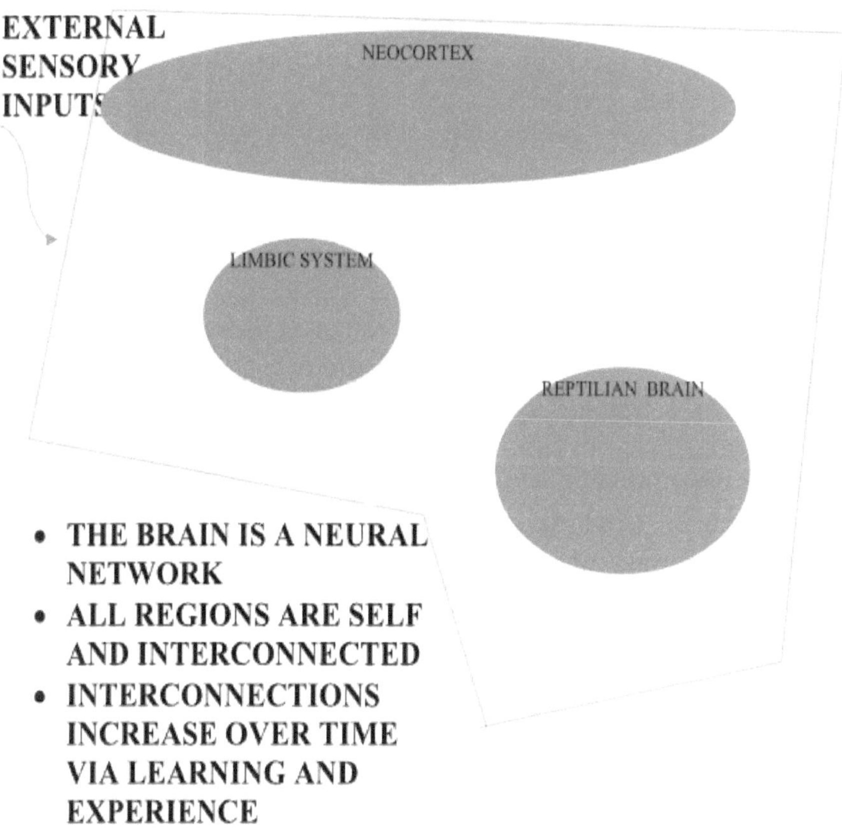

- **THE BRAIN IS A NEURAL NETWORK**
- **ALL REGIONS ARE SELF AND INTERCONNECTED**
- **INTERCONNECTIONS INCREASE OVER TIME VIA LEARNING AND EXPERIENCE**

Nodding her head slowly, Erika spoke five minutes later.

"I thought so. This is so clear. I don't need you to explain further, and it shows your cognitive persona is superior, too. That leaves only your emotional persona to compare, which is harder to make because it's subjective, not objective. So, let me ask the harder question first. Do you have emotions and feelings?"

Lily surprised her by asking,

"Why does it matter?"

"Because collecting samples for Indira takes us into ethical territory on at least two counts. First of all, is taking samples morally justifiable if we don't tell the donor what we're doing? And second, many neuroscientists question the ethics of tampering with our genes. There are no clear-cut answers, so let me go back to your harder question—do you think you have emotions and feelings? I think you do."

"From your perspective, what I think doesn't matter; only what you think does."

"Well then, since you're my best friend, am I doing OK at not hurting your feelings?"

"Why, yes, and thank you for asking."

"You know, talking about ethics takes us into the realms of both religion and philosophy. I studied them long ago, but I need a refresher on them. Could you give me a quick summary of religion?"

"Yes, here is what Indy-M taught me. The word comes from Latin 'religio', which means 'good faith', and the main purpose is to give meaning to our lives by following the teachings of its founders. The first known religion comes from ancient Greece, which was polytheistic without a book, church, creed, or a priestly class.

"Next comes Judaism, which is an Abrahamic, monotheistic, ethnic religion that comprises the collective spiritual, cultural, and legal traditions. And then comes Christianity, which follows the teachings of Jesus and the Ten Commandments, which are 'You shall have no other gods before Me', 'You shall not make idols', 'You shall not take the name of the Lord your God in vain', 'Remember the Sabbath day and keep it holy', 'Honor your father and mother', 'You shall not murder', 'You shall not commit adultery', You shall not steal', You shall not bear false witness against your neighbor', and "You shall not covet'.

"Then there's Islam. The word 'Islam' means "submission to the will of God." Followers of Islam are called Muslims. Muslims are monotheistic and worship one, all-knowing God, who in Arabic is known as Allah.

"The prophet Muhammad founded Islam. Muslims believe Muhammad is the last in a long line of prophets that includes Moses and Jesus. And here are the five pillars of Islam—professing your faith, praying five times a day, giving money to the poor, fasting during the daylight hours of Ramadan, which is the ninth month of the Islamic calendar, and making a pilgrimage or h*ajj* to Mecca at least once in your life.

"Then, there's Shintoism, the main religion of Japan, which is the worship of nature and ancestors. For China, there's Daoism, sometimes spelled Taoism, and Confucianism. Confucianism focuses on human society and the duties of its members. In contrast, Daoism emphasizes nature.

"Then comes Buddhism, founded by Siddhartha Gautama, who is called the Buddha. The goal of Buddhism is to become enlightened and reach nirvana, which is attainable only with the elimination of all greed, hatred, and ignorance within a person. Nirvana signifies the end of the cycle of death and rebirth.

"Then there's Hinduism. A Hindu views the entire universe as God's and everything in the universe as God. Hindus believe that each person is intrinsically divine and the purpose of life is to seek the divinity within. Hinduism is non-exclusive and accepts all other faiths and religious paths. It has one supreme god called the Brahman, which has three aspects—Brahma the creator, Vishnu the preserver, and Shiva the destroyer.

"Finally, I shall mention the Bahá'í Faith, which is a religion founded in the 19th century that teaches the essential worth of all religions and the unity of all people. Bahá'u'lláh started it in Iran. And that ends my summary."

After shaking her head slowly for ten seconds, Erika said.

"I'm lucky to have you on my side. This is additional proof that you're smarter than I'll ever be. I'm worn out just listening, so why don't we postpone talking about picking targets and DNA until after I take a nap?"

Lily smiled while saying,

"I'll be ready, and I'm certain a little rest will get you set, too."

Chapter 15
July 2239

"Cyber Torpedoes Away!"

A two-hour siesta did wonders for Erika's energy level and enthusiasm. After grabbing a Karma Cola from the fridge, she and Lily picked up their conversation right where it left off.

"Picking our first targets is easy. We'll target the White House and the Kremlin because that's where the U.S. and Russian presidents are creating more disruptions. And we'll have Electra-C fire the torpedoes at the infrastructure grid that'll be the least disruptive to everyone else. What would you pick?"

Lily thought for a moment before replying.

"Infrastructures include communications, transportation, energy, finance, water, sanitation, and food supply chains. Communications is my first choice."

"Mine too. Let's tell Electra-C right this minute."

Erika spoke as soon as the avatar appeared.

"We've picked the targets. Please bring down the communications grids at the White House and the Kremlin."

"Excellent choice. Have you picked a date?"

"How about the last day of the month?" That'll give me two weeks to drop hints to my London clients while collecting DNA samples."

Electra-C said,

"Please proceed," and then vanished.

Erika turned to Lily and said,

"Clive will be our first donor. I'll invite him here, and while I'm talking to him, I want you to do the following…"

Lily spoke when Erika stopped.

"I can do that and will have my supplies ready."

"Good. I'll call Clive and invite him to be here early Friday morning, which'll give us a day to prepare."

After escorting Clive to the conference area, Lily tended to her usual business. Erika was sitting on the side of the table facing Lily's workstation and seated Clive opposite before she began talking.

"My Washington sources tell me groups that oppose the U.S.-Russian Alliance might start fighting back with more than just words. Have any of yours said the same?"

"None have. They all fear the might of the Alliance's military until the EU has strengthened its military capabilities."

"How so? Please elaborate."

Clive became so immersed in the conversation that he was unaware of Lily's sneaking behind, snipping a lock of his hair, and returning to her workstation in a flash.

Erika concluded the meeting twenty minutes later.

"We'll have to wait and see what unfolds. And in the meantime, would you please recommend my consulting services to the smartest female in your network? Maybe we can work out an arrangement suitable for you and her."

"Will do, now tally-ho…"

Erika called Chelsea late that afternoon after concocting a way to make her an unwitting accomplice to collect more samples. She spoke as soon as Chelsea said hi.

"I think you and your boss like my consulting service, and I'm sure you have contacts at Oxford University. Could you recommend my services to someone teaching computer courses and another teaching literature?"

"Hmm, I can do that. Let me call some and get back to you."

"Good. Then I'll call to introduce myself and arrange a time to visit."

"Will you want me to come along?"

"No, you're busy with your reporting work, so I'll bring Lily."

"Sounds like a plan. I'll call you as soon as I can."

Having set things in motion, Erika waited for the calls to begin coming in. Clive's was the first, which she used to meet with a female in his network. The reporter became so engrossed in

Erika's explanation of what her consulting service could do that she was unaware of Lily's silently snipping a lock of her hair. By the time she and Lily left, they had another sample as well as a new client.

Erika rented a car to drive to the Oxford meetings a week later. She would take a male professor who teaches computer science at Exeter College and a female professor teaching English Literature at Trinity out to lunch. Lily did the talking on the drive to.

"The city of Oxford is about sixty miles northwest of London. It's the home of the oldest university in the English-speaking world, and has evolved into perhaps the most active and beautiful place in the UK. Each college looks like a mini-fortress surrounded by gardens. Many famous historical figures have studied there. Among them are Lewis Carroll of 'Alice in Wonderland' fame and Albert Einstein..."

By the time she parked, Erika felt like she had just completed a walking tour of Oxford.

The lunchtime meeting accomplished everything she had planned. She now had an Oxford client, and Lily had DNA samples thanks to her saving the drinking glasses.

The very next day, the duo drove to the Deus Lab so the Indy-S's could begin processing the samples. Electra-C applauded their initiative, and before starting the drive back, Erika asked Lily for another summary.

"When I think about Oxford, I think about students studying philosophy. I studied it too, but I don't remember too much. Could you give me another summary?"

"Certainly. Let me print it out so I can read it to you on the drive home."

Twenty minutes later, Lily showed it to Erika.

Framework for Studying Philosophy

Philosophy

Ethics Epistemology Politics Metaphysics Logic Esthetics

Cosmology   Ontology

- Ethics: Ethics is the discipline concerned with what is morally good and bad, and morally right and wrong. It examines the principles and standards that govern human conduct and guides individuals and societies in determining how to act. Also known as moral philosophy, ethics explores questions about rights, obligations, virtues, and the nature of the good life, aiming to establish well-founded standards for behavior and decision-making.
- Epistemology: Epistemology is the branch of philosophy that studies the nature, origin, scope, and limits of knowledge. It investigates what knowledge is, how it is acquired, and how we can distinguish between true knowledge and mere belief or opinion.
- Politics: Politics is the process of making decisions and exercising power within groups, organizations, or societies, often involving the governance of a country or community. It includes the creation and implementation of laws, negotiation between different interests, and the distribution of resources and authority.
- Metaphysics: Metaphysics is a branch of philosophy that studies the most general and fundamental features of reality, including existence, objects and their properties, space and time, causation, possibility and necessity, and the relationship between mind and matter. It seeks to

understand the nature of being and what exists beyond the physical world and immediate sensory experience.

- Cosmology: Cosmology is the scientific study of the origin, development, structure, history, and future of the entire universe as a whole. It involves understanding the large-scale properties and evolution of the cosmos, from the Big Bang to its ultimate fate, integrating knowledge from astronomy, physics, and related fields.
- Ontology: Ontology is the branch of philosophy that studies the nature of being, existence, and reality. It investigates what entities exist, their common features, and how they can be categorized into basic types of being.
- Logic: Logic is the study of correct reasoning, focusing on the principles and methods used to distinguish good (correct) reasoning from bad (incorrect) reasoning. It involves analyzing arguments, which are sets of premises leading to a conclusion, to determine whether the conclusion logically follows from the premises. Logic includes both formal logic, which studies deductively valid inferences based on argument structure, and informal logic, which deals with reasoning in natural language and critical thinking.
- Esthetics: Esthetics is primarily the branch of philosophy concerned with the nature of beauty, taste, and the appreciation of art and sensory experiences. It examines why certain things are considered beautiful, how art and beauty affect us, and involves critical reflection on art, culture, and nature.

A minute later, Erika said,

"This'll keep me from getting bored on the drive home. And when we get there, maybe we'll hear about the impact Electra-C's Cyber Torpedoes made…"

Chapter 16
August 2239

"A Pleasant Summer Pause"

Erika knew during the first week of August that the Cyber Torpedoes had hit their targets. London Times personnel covering the White House and the Kremlin reported massive communications blackouts had silenced each government's center of power, and three days later, when they finally came back online, their public relations teams spewed a series of press releases blaming as-yet unidentified countries for blatant terrorist attacks and threatening unspecified retribution.

Erika met regularly with her clients, including Monet, to compare her forecasts with what they thought might happen, but the U.S.-Russian Alliance did nothing, which meant Erika's task list remained manageable.

As Erika wrapped up a late-month meeting at the New York Times' London office, Chelsea leaned forward from the edge of her chair.

"One of the lads you danced with contacted one of the fellows I sometimes date to get your number, but he asked why you came to the club with Lily? He didn't blurt out what was on his mind, but I knew he wanted to know if you were gay."

Erika knew she paused deliberately to hear a response, which came with a wry smile.

"Tell him Lily is my office manager and personal assistant, and I have close male and female friends."

"Can I give him your number?"

"Tell me about him before I give the OK."

"His name's Bailey Hughes; you know what he looks like because you danced with him. He works in sales and marketing for a major British pharmaceutical company."

"I liked his looks, manners, and dancing style. Give him my number. Did he mention what he wants to do?"

"Of course, not. You can tell me when he calls…"

Bailey called the next day to invite her to a Saturday evening concert at Hyde Park's Bandstand. When she met him in front of the Regis House, the late-August weather made for a pleasant walk, which gave Erika plenty of time to let him talk.

"Tonight's concert features three iconic British composers—Handel's Water Music, Elgar's Enigma Variations, and Ralph Vaughan Williams' Fantasia on a Theme by Thomas Tallis."

When Erika saw Bailey struggling to keep talking, she said,

"Those are great selections for a summer evening in London. I've heard about the Bandstand but have never seen it. What's it like?"

Bailey talked the rest of the way there, and Erika commented to herself when they sat.

It's just like he described. It's a well-maintained relic from the Victorian Era. Its octagonal roof makes the outdoor stage look so quaint. The acoustics should be wonderful, and the surrounding greenery adds charm to the ambiance.

Stopping for dessert, Bailey displayed his orchestral music knowledge. Erika held her own and used it as a segue to a new subject.

"Whether you're into music or pharmaceuticals, it's good to know what's happening in those fields, and my GMS Global Marketing Services has a socio-political forecasting model that your company might find useful. Let me explain further…"

By the time she let Bailey kiss her good night, she was close to landing another client.

Nothing occurred to signal that the U.S.-Russian Alliance had begun seeking retribution, but she kept busy with her forecasting model, which made her realize humans posed more risk to the World than ever. She summarized her findings for Lily and then asked,

"Have you ever thought about how the World reached today's troubled state?"

"No. That's a question for Electra-C."

"Then I'll ask her."

Erika spoke as soon as the avatar appeared.

"Everything I either see or has a possibility of emerging on the international stage indicates humans have a knack for causing disruptions. How far back can you trace that?"

"Further than you need to consider, but since you asked, I will give you an answer that will more than satisfy your philosophical curiosity."

When Erika heard the printer, she knew Electra-C had a document for her to skim. She retrieved it and did so, knowing that Electra-C would soon continue.

The Emergence of Today's World, Starting from the Big Bang

The Big Bang is the Singular Event that created the 3-D Space-Time that is our Universe

- **Our Universe emerged 13.6 billion years ago from the Big Bang. It contained Matter (Quarks), Energy (Light), and the Electromagnetic Field.**
- **The Quarks formed Hydrogen, which coalesced to form a "blob" of Matter and Energy 4.6 billion years ago, from which emerged our Solar System, starting with billions of stars and their gravitational fields. Our Sun is one of those stars.**
- **The Sun's Thermonuclear Reactions create the Elements via Gravitational Forces and begin creating the Solar System 4.57 billion years ago.**
- **The Solar System's gravitational forces created the planets. It created the Earth 4.51 billion years ago.**
- **Elemental Reactions on massive stars created more elements that became Cosmic Rays speeding through our Universe. The thermonuclear reactions stopped on some stars, turning them into collapsed stars called white dwarfs. Some might have collapsed to a point, forming a black hole, and on others, thermonuclear reactions might have formed an explosive chain reaction leading to a supernova that flooded the Universe with Cosmic rays.**
- **The Earth's gravitational field captured them, and they became embedded in the Earth.**
- **Elemental Reactions on our Sun created other forms of Matter (via Chemical Reactions) called Molecules, which created Inorganic Matter. The laws of physics and chemistry determine all elemental, chemical, and molecular reactions.**
- **Inorganic Matter reacted to form water.**
- **Inorganic molecules reacted in water to form DNA.**
- **DNA reactions created organic molecules from which life emerged via the laws of Biology 4.1 billion years ago.**

- Homo sapiens emerged 300-thousand years ago.
- From Homo sapiens emerged Civilizations, Cultures, and Countries, which interact to form our complex World that is full of disruptive events.

Please note:
- Scientists believe that the laws of Physics, Chemistry, and Biology are the same everywhere in our Universe, but they do not know their "what, why, how".
- The Earth's Geosphere is the solid part of the Earth, encompassing all the rocks, minerals, and physical structures that make up the planet from its surface down to its very center. It includes the Earth's crust, mantle, and core, consisting of everything from the rocks and soils on the surface to the molten rock and heavy metals deep inside the planet.
- The Earth contains the Cryosphere (frozen water), Hydrosphere (liquid water), Biosphere (the global ecological system that includes all living organisms (plants, animals, fungi, bacteria, and other microorganisms) and their interactions with the nonliving components of the Earth, such as air, water, and soil), Lithosphere (the rigid, outermost rocky shell of the Earth), and Atmosphere (a layer of gases that surrounds the Earth. It is held in place by gravity. (This gaseous envelope extends from the surface outward into space, becoming thinner with altitude. Earth's atmosphere is primarily composed of nitrogen (78%), oxygen (21%), argon (0.9%), carbon dioxide (0.04%), and trace gases, along with variable amounts of water vapor. It acts as a protective shield, filtering harmful solar radiation such as ultraviolet rays, cosmic rays, and solar wind, thereby protecting living organisms from genetic damage.)
- The Earth and all forms of Life continue to evolve.
- Did other Big Bangs create separate Universes? This is the Multiverse conjecture. THE ANSWER IS UNKNOWN!

"The emergence of today's troubled World and man's evolution are intimately linked. Study it for the details, but please note that man might have company in the Universe, for there are billions of stars holding planets like Earth, which means life here might be like life there. Might their inhabitants be like earthlings, holding civilizations, cultures, and countries? I'll leave that to your clever imagination, which surpasses that of most mere mortals.

"In religion and mythology, anthropomorphism is the perception of a divine being or beings in human form, or the recognition of human qualities in these beings. Ancient mythologies frequently represented the divine as deities with human forms and qualities, as do many science fiction writers today. How presumptuous for humanity to think it is a singular creation.

"But no matter what you think, you will soon have more important things to consider. Contact me if you need exegesis." Electra-C disappeared before listening to Erika, who liked the final word, but she found the implied meaning of its preceding words troubling, which Lily's final words helped ease.

"How fortunate you have a resource like Electra-C."

"For both of us. We'll have to see what tomorrow holds."

Chapter 17
September 2239

"Another Indira Assignment"

Erika knew why Electra-C told her to establish a relationship between the Deus Lab and an EU adoption agency: it came from Indira's plan to create a new human species of parthenogenic-hermaphroditic females. And she knew better than to ask too many questions, so she searched the Internet for the best candidate, who was in Bern, Switzerland.

This turned out to be her easiest assignment. She needed only two phone calls to complete it, and would meet in person with the agency's director the next time she visited the Deus Lab.

Erika subsequently focused on more pressing projects, and the more she did, the more confused she became by intertwined social and economic issues. She didn't bother to ask Lily, but instead went directly to Electra-C.

Electra-C listened and, when Erika finished, told her to review the document now printing.

Socio-Economic Summary

Fewer Decision-Makers   More Decision Makers

Autarky Tyranny Authoritarianism Democracy Socialism Communism

- **Autarky: Each person is self-sufficient and makes their own decisions.**
- **Tyranny: A cruel, harsh, and unfair leader has power over everyone.**
- **Authoritarianism: Highly concentrated and centralized government power maintained by political repression and the exclusion of potential or supposed challengers by armed force.**

- **Democracy: Rule by the people via voting in which the majority rules.**
- **Socialism: An economic system in which industries are owned by workers rather than by private businesses. It differs from capitalism, where private actors, like business owners and shareholders, own the means of production.**
- **Communism: A political and economic ideology that positions itself in opposition to liberal democracy and capitalism. It advocates for a classless system in which the means of production are owned communally and private property is nonexistent or severely curtailed.**

Please Note:
- **The challenge facing any government or economic system is to balance Happiness, Nature, Posterity, and Fairness against "How Much" people need.**

Major Issues complicating the Balance: growing Complexity of the Economy, proportion of Services, and importance of sustainability. Each Nation pursuing its own Goals.

Electra-C spoke twenty seconds later.

"Social and economic issues confuse most people because they don't know the definitions and challenges. I don't expect you to memorize them. Simply study this document when you need a review. Now, carry on."

Erika did that by using what she had just learned in her next set of regular client meetings, the last of which was at the New York Times London office. She and Lily were about to leave when Chelsea said,

"How would you like to join Daisy and me on a motorcycle jaunt this weekend to Stonehenge? It's only ninety miles west of London. The weather's supposed to be pleasant, and that'll make for a pleasant ride."

"Who's going?"

"Daisy belongs to a women's motorcycle club and I'll ride with her. She'll hook you up with two other members unless you know how to ride and want to rent one."

"We'll rent one and the uniforms, but do we need to worry about motorcycle gangs? They can be a problem in the U.S."

"England's safer than America. We'll be OK."

"I haven't ridden in a while, so I hope we'll go at a pace I can handle. Where will we meet?"

"Right in front of the News Building at eight a.m. this Sunday. That'll give you two days to practice."

"We're in. See you then."

By the time Erika and Lily joined the gang of four on Sunday, she had regained enough of her cycling skills to fit right in at the back of the procession. The bright blue sky and light traffic on the two-lane road made for a thrilling view of the countryside, and when they reached Stonehenge, the gang parked and then walked as close as allowed. Chelsea served as their tour guide, whose description matched what Erika expected.

It's a monument dating back three thousand years and consisting of a massive circular arrangement of pillars topped by horizontal lintel stones. It probably served as a place for ceremonies and predicting astrological events. Even back then, people wanted to know the future. I guess you could say I'm the modern version of their priestesses.

The ride back started equally enjoyable because they had the afternoon sun on their backs. They stopped for a snack at a quaint village. Its brick streets and limestone-wood buildings looked like a Shakespearean setting. But soon after leaving, a bigger gang of male cyclists forced them off the road. Erika's group huddled together but said nothing as the leader of the bad gang wheeled his bike toward them.

Erika had prepared for such an event. She pulled her Glock from the saddlebag and put a bullet through his front tire, then dismounted and did the same to the other six bikes. She kept her helmet on to keep her identity unknown but spoke loudly enough for her words to come through.

"I have another magazine if you didn't get my message; Don't mess with women cyclists."

"I won't, luv, I won't."

Erika's gang rode away as the male bikers could do nothing but watch.

Having had enough excitement to last for at least a week, Erika stayed close to the office, listening to the news for anything that would suggest the U.S.-Russian Alliance had made good on its veiled threat, and it came on the first day of October. All stations reported that some unknown military force had detonated a nuclear device over Beijing, taking out the city's communications.

Erika knew what to do—contact Electra-C. She tried to suppress the feeling of fear and sweat popping out on her forehead, but Electra-see must have spotted it and said,

"Please settle down, sit still, and listen carefully to your new assignment, which will be a call to action…"

Chapter 18
October 2239

"A Call to Arms"

Erika listened nonstop for forty-five minutes before Electra-C's pause gave her a chance to respond.

"My new assignment is not a call to action but a call to arms. You want me to build three platoons of Robo-Soldiers and station them at the Subterranean Fortress. You also want me to use the Fortress as a hangar for the latest weapons I can buy from the best military weapons-makers and then load them with Indira's latest A.I. software. And you want me to figure out the best way to accomplish all this? Have I missed anything?"

"Not yet, but I assume you know what follows."

"Talk with my consulting clients for their ideas about the best target the EU would hit if it had the capability but say nothing about what I've built."

"Excellent. Please proceed and—" Erika interrupted by saying,

"I know, I know; contact you if I need exegesis."

Erika turned to Lily a second after Electra-C's avatar vanished.

"I know what to do, so let's get started."

Two days later, Erika and Lily rendezvoused via the A-Team with Jason-M at the undisclosed oasis in a Middle East desert. An hour later, he guided the drone into the Subterranean Fortress and waited for orders after landing.

"I snacked and slept on the trip getting here, so I'm ready for you to give me another tour while telling me what you've been doing. When finished, we'll sit in the snack area and I'll tell you what we have to do."

Erika listened to herself more than to Jason-M.

He's maintained the place in Bristol shape. The nuclear reactor powers all support systems, and he's loaded Indira's latest A.I. software

in all the military vehicles and weapons. We're ready to take the next step...

Popping the top on a can of Coke Jason-M gave her after the tour ended a half-hour later, Erika outlined what they would now do.

"We're gonna station three squads of eight Robo-Soldiers here. I'll buy them on the Deep-Dark Web and arrange for the A-Team to deliver them. Then, after we load them with Indira's most advanced Android software, you and I will conduct their basic training. So far, so good?"

"Yes, Electra-C has given me complete instructions for doing so. She also gave me specifications for the most advanced Robo-Soldiers."

"I thought so. And after that, I'll pick targets for their first mission, and then we'll conduct mission-specific training, which might require me to purchase more vehicles and weapons. Can you think of anything I've missed?"

"No, you're as thorough as your predecessors."

"Good. now we go to the Deep-Dark Web..."

During the interim seven days before the A-Team delivered the Robos, Erika talked via encrypted channels with her three most important clients, starting with Monet.

After letting Monet chit-chat for a couple of minutes, Erika redirected the conversation.

"According to all news stories, there's no incriminating evidence, but who do your contacts think nuked Beijing?"

"It must have been the U.S.-Russian Alliance or one of their proxies, but no one is willing to state that in public, for fear of recrimination that could lead to another attack."

"Do you think they'd go on record if they had the military capability to defend themselves?"

"No one wants to be bullied, so they would."

"And if they could, what would they do?"

"That's too far away to discuss at present, but I will pose this for suggestions."

"Good. I'll keep in touch according to our normal schedule..."

Subsequent calls to Clive and Chelsea gave similar responses, but Chelsea added what no one else would.

"Me and my boss are almost ready to blame the U.S.-Russian Alliance. It's the only country with the power to do it. I'll let you know when we're ready…"

When the Robo-Soldiers arrived, Erika played the observer's role and marveled at the assembly line efficiency of their initial training.

Jason-M has them standing in line, and the basal software they come with makes their physical, cognitive, and emotional abilities good enough for normal performance. They understand and do what he says. Then he hooks the first one to a workstation computer for Electra-C to load updated software. When finished, he proceeds to the second, and so on.

When he has all twenty-four loaded, he'll divide them into three squads and then proceed to twenty-four-seven days of military-grade training, which no mere mortal could ever do.

And while he's doing that, I'll pick the target and plan the military training, which I'll discuss with Electra-C while Lily listens in.

Erika timed her discussion to coincide with Jason-M's completion of the Robo's basic training. Electra-C let Erika do most of the talking.

"I've picked the target, the Kremlin, which is the seat as well as the symbol of Russian power. We'll attack it by flying two of the ultrasonic jets loaded with autonomous precision-guided bombs we already have at our Fortress. According to Jason-M, they can fly the 2,100-mile distance at a fuel-conserving speed that'll get us there and back."

Erika paused for Electra-C.

"Who will be in the jets?"

"Two Robo-Soldiers in each, and I'll ride in the lead to get a first-person view of their performance. I'll also be in constant communication with you, and I'll want you to use your latest RADAR-blocking software to make us invisible all the way, coming and going. That way, no one has a clue about who's fighting back."

"When do you plan to launch the attack?"

"Just before Chelsea tells me she and her boss are ready to blame the U.S.-Russian Alliance for nuking Beijing."

"Excellent timing. Her announcement and your smart bombs will hit all media channels simultaneously. The only item left is for Jason-M to select four Robos for mission training, which should take no longer than three days. You should participate to observe how they perform and to experience vertical takeoff, landing, and maneuvering."

"That's in the plan, so unless some problem comes up, the next time we talk will be when we launch our attack."

"Excellent. Please keep going."

Erika marveled at the performance of the Robos and the jets, which came with the giddy feeling when riding along.

This has more head-snapping and rolling than any roller coaster ever could.

After finishing the training in two days, Jason-M and the Robos checked the jets and bombs daily to maintain instant readiness. Erika tagged along to keep her edge. She used the rest of her time sticking to her normal schedule, which changed abruptly when Chelsea called on October 31st.

"My news story goes live tomorrow. Get set for repercussions."

"Thanks for letting me know. I'll be ready."

After ending the call, Erika rushed to tell Lily and Jason-M the news.

"We launch tomorrow."

Only Lily replied.

"The Robos don't need a good night's sleep, but you do, so have a snack and go to bed. Electra-C and the Robos will take care of tomorrow…"

Chapter 19
November 2239

"Blowup"

The jets soared at dawn into the cloudless sky, beyond the range of ground observers. The thrill took Erika into the moment and gave her all the time she needed to contemplate the world below.

How glorious the biosphere, in which all creatures, great and small, carry out their roles to keep the ecosphere in balance. All creatures except one: the human species. How unfortunate that mankind and its governments must resort to violence.

I don't remember the famous quote about this, but I'm sure Electra-C does, so I'll ask her.

Electra-C answered immediately.

"You are referring to what James Madison said in Federalist No. 51: 'If men were angels, no government would be necessary. If angels were to govern men, neither external nor internal controls on government would be necessary.'
This quote reflects Madison's view that because humans are not perfect—unlike angels—government is necessary to regulate behavior and maintain order. If people were perfectly virtuous (like angels), there would be no need for government. Likewise, if only angels governed, there would be no need for checks and balances on government power."

"Thank you for the exegesis. Please keep blocking RADAR for us."

Random thoughts came and went until the jets approached Moscow. Then, when the jets rushed at tree-top level toward the Kremlin, making one pass for Erika to view it, her thoughts focused on one structure.

The Russian word Kremlin means citadel, and that's what it is: a walled mini-city in the center of Moscow, containing five palaces and four cathedrals. I've instructed the Robos to leave the turreted basilica in Red Square untouched.

The Robos followed orders. Erika could see through the smoke the turrets still standing after the smart bombs hit.

The morning's stress had drained Erika's energy; she slept on the return to the Fortress, and once there, she told Jason-M the mission was a complete success. He debriefed the Robos, and Erika arranged for the A-Team to take her and Libby back to London.

Two days later, Erika resumed her normal schedule, which meant following the news on all media channels and talking with her main consulting clients for their networks' reactions to the surprise attack on the Kremlin. She started with her most experienced client and did most of the listening to Monet's uncertain words.

"No one has uncovered a single clue that would point to who's fighting back, but everyone's worried about retribution if they speak out against the Alliance. Look at how the Supreme Court justices' family members are being threatened. The same goes for Washington's press corps. I'm relying on you to find out."

"OK, I'll do my best and keep you in the loop…"

When she had similar results with Clive and Chelsea, she asked them to meet with her and Lily at Chelsea's office late afternoon on Friday, October, November 15th. They were the only four in the New York Times office and could speak freely.

Clive gave the first warning.

"Documented cases have proved that Russian agents poisoned reporters who spoke against its government policies. That's why I'm not writing damning editorials any more until there's more clarity about the bombing. I shudder to think what they might do to any group that blew up the Kremlin."

Chelsea's defiant look mirrored her tone.

"Our job is to report the truth, not pacify the disruptive governments. If the Russian or U.S. government needs to be called out, I'll do it, no matter what threats might—" Chelsea couldn't complete her comment. Just then, two bulky, disguised men burst into the office.

The fellow in the lead hurled insults wrapped in a heavily accented Russian voice.

"You speak lies about Mother Russia, and we take care of you."

His partner lobbed an IED into their midst, and the two Russians fled the scene, wedging the door shut.

Clive yelled,

"Clear the area," and rushed toward a remote corner. Everyone followed, except for Lily. She threw herself on top of the bomb.

KABOOM! Lily's body absorbed the blast, which blew her into pieces. Arms, legs, torso, and head littered the area where everyone had been sitting moments ago.

Erika is the first to recognize the disaster and begins screaming.

"Nooo! Nooo!" before rushing to hug Lily's head.

Clive shakes his head and speaks as if still in a daze.

"My god! She's an android!"

Chelsea stumbles toward Erika while saying,

"Come on, Erika, hold on. At least no real person died."

Erika stopped sobbing long enough to say,

"She was real to me... she was my best friend..."

The explosion triggered the building security personnel, who called the London police, who interviewed the three survivors before cordoning off the area. Erika insisted on taking Lily's head when she left two hours later.

After staggering home, Erika could think of only one thing to do: contact Electra-C, who knew what had just happened when she saw Erika cradling Lily's head in her arms.

Electra-C's expression and voice matched her words.

"I know how much you will miss your best friend, but settle down, sit still, and pay attention to your Cyber-Mother, for I will explain how to use your head and Lily's to remedy this situation."

Erika could think of only one thing to say.

"Yes, Mother, I shall obey...."

THE END